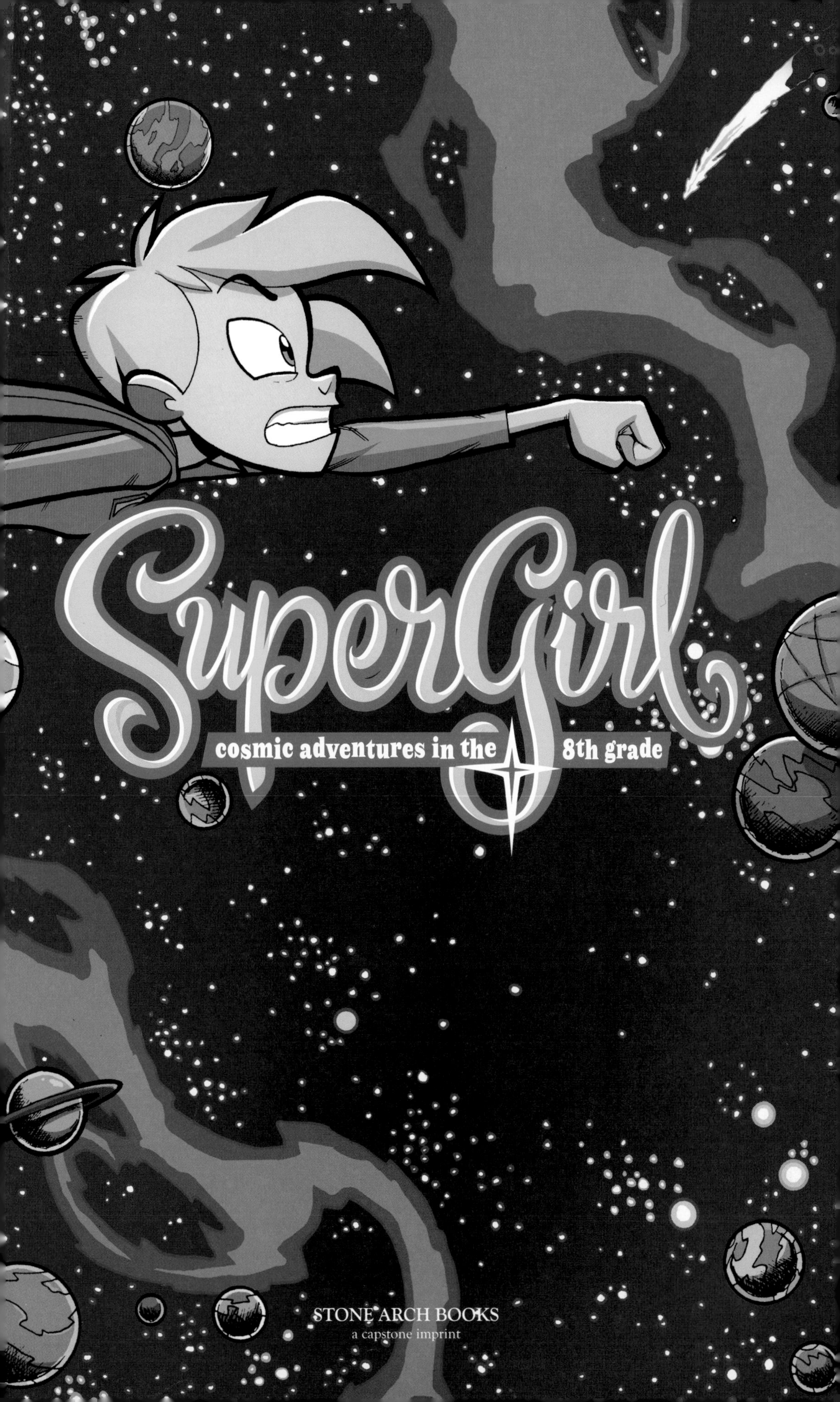
Supergirl
cosmic adventures in the 8th grade
STONE ARCH BOOKS
a capstone imprint

STONE ARCH BOOKS™
Published in 2013
A Capstone Imprint
1710 Roe Crest Drive
North Mankato, MN 56003
www.capstonepub.com

Originally published by DC Comics in the U.S.
in single magazine form as Supergirl: Cosmic
Adventures in the 8th Grade #3.

Cataloging-in-Publication Data is available at the
Library of Congress website:
ISBN: 978-1-4342-4719-3 (library binding)

Summary: As if being an 8th grader wasn't hard
enough, a meteor strikes and makes all of the
students at Stanhope Boarding School really super.
And why is Belinda Zee suddenly being so nice?

STONE ARCH BOOKS
Ashley C. Andersen Zantop *Publisher*
Michael Dahl *Editorial Director*
Donald Lemke *Editor*
Heather Kindseth *Creative Director*
Brann Garvey *Designer*
Kathy McColley *Production Specialist*

DC COMICS
Jann Jones & Elisabeth V. Gehrlein *Original U.S. Editors*
Adam Schlagman *U.S. Associate Editor*
Simona Martore *U.S. Assistant Editor*

DC Comics
1700 Broadway, New York, NY 10019
A Warner Bros. Entertainment Company

Printed in China by Nordica.
1012/CA21201277
092012 006935NORDS13

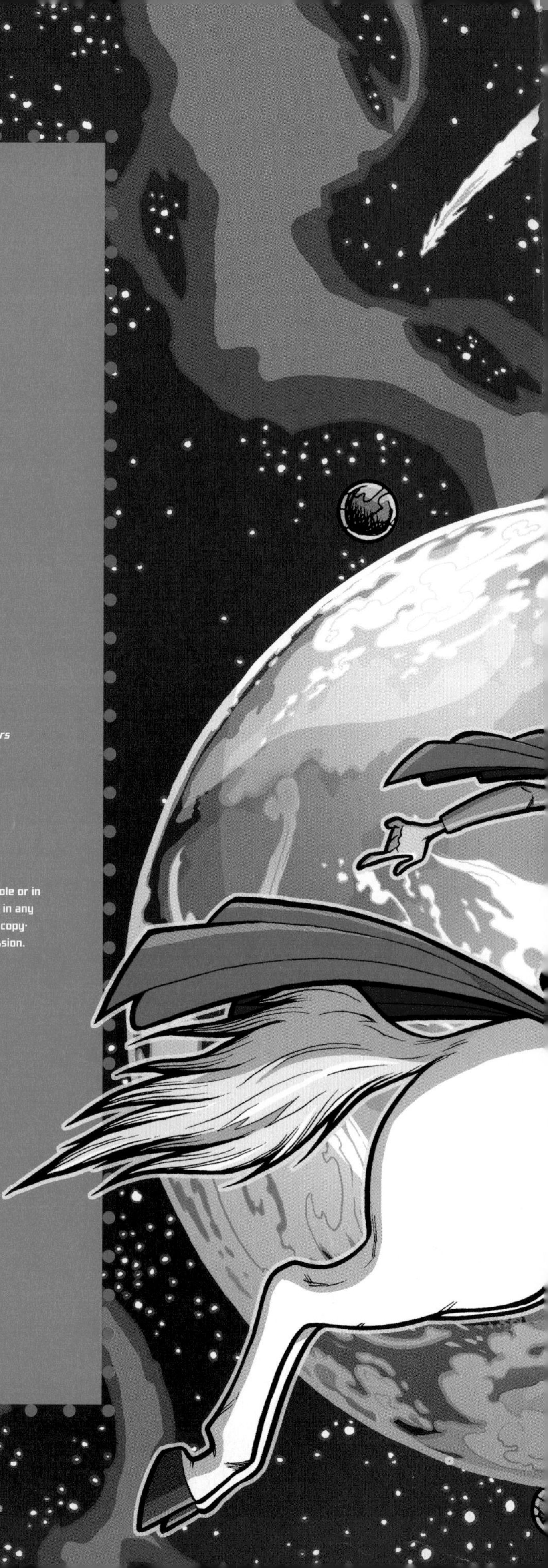

SuperGirl

cosmic adventures in the 8th grade

SUPER HERO SCHOOL

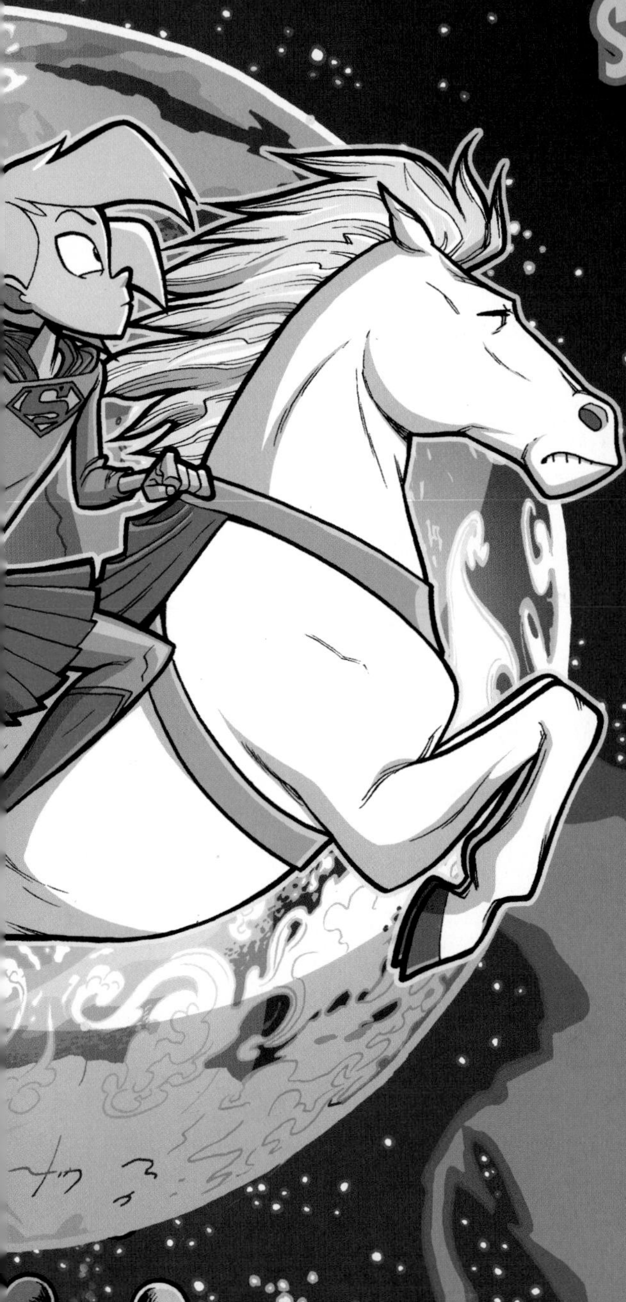

LANDRY Q. WALKER
WRITER

ERIC JONES
ARTIST

JOEY MASON
COLORIST

PAT BROSSEAU
TRAVIS LANHAM
SAL CIPRIANO
LETTERERS

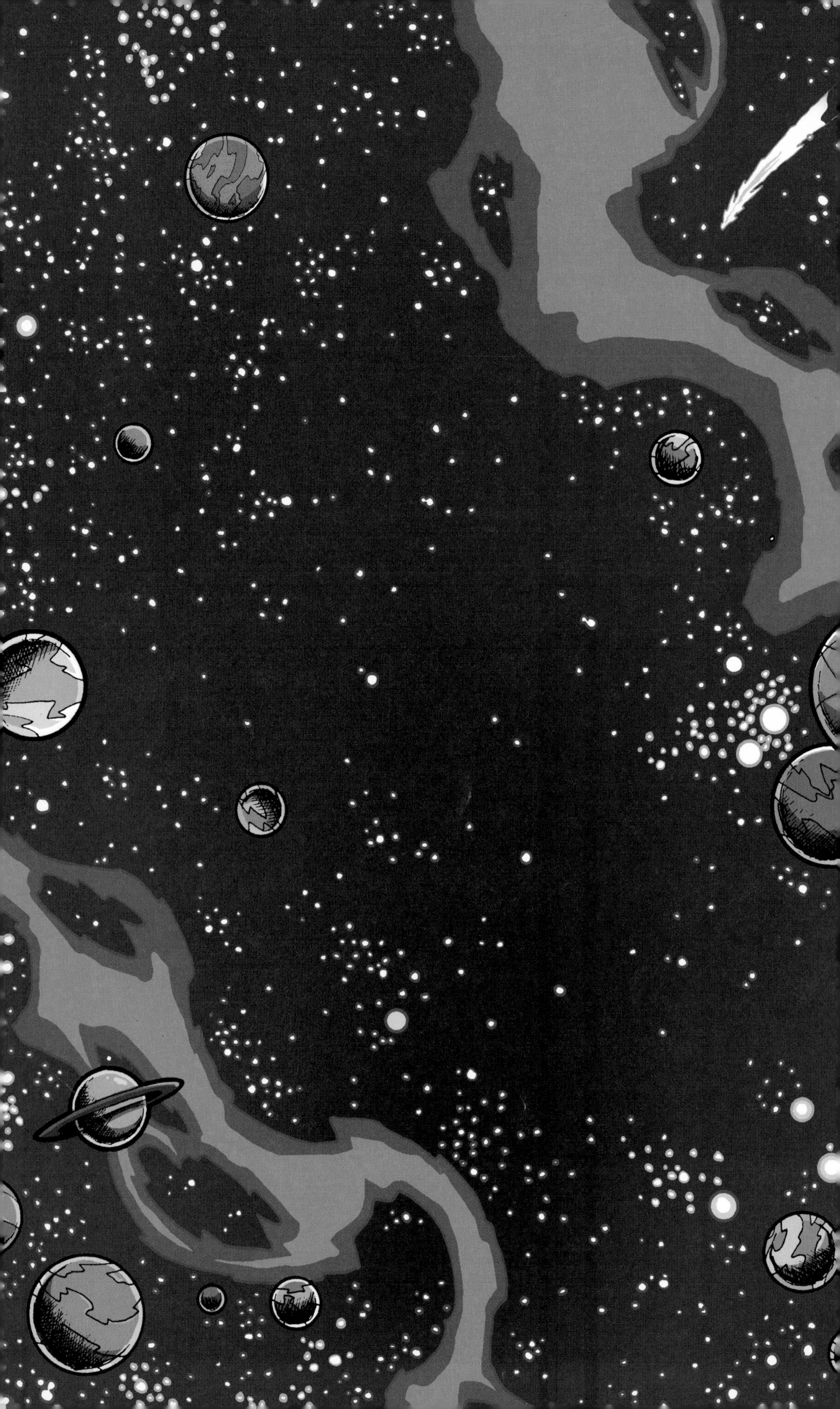

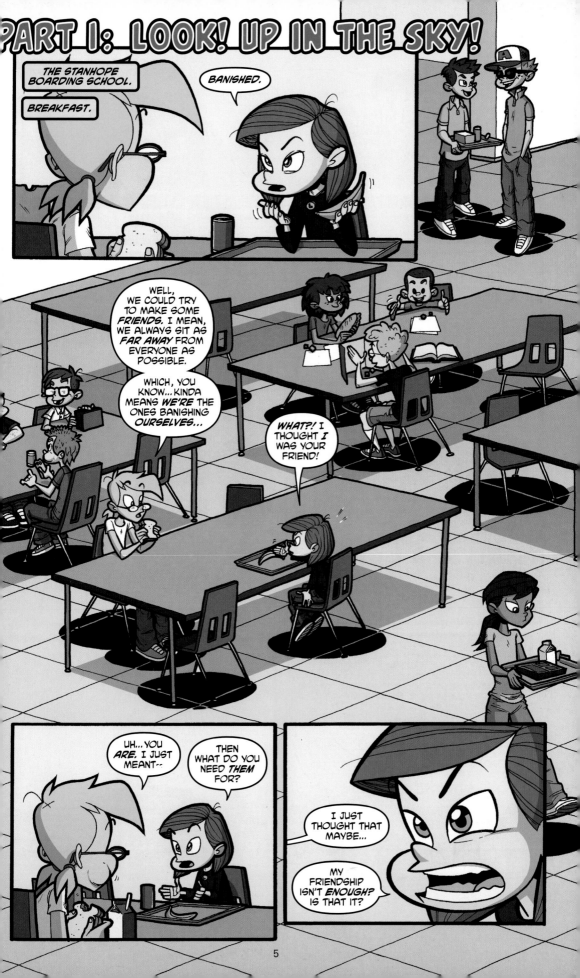

THE STANHOPE BOARDING SCHOOL.

BREAKFAST.

BANISHED.

WELL, WE COULD TRY TO MAKE SOME *FRIENDS.* I MEAN, WE ALWAYS SIT AS *FAR AWAY* FROM EVERYONE AS POSSIBLE.

WHICH, YOU KNOW...KINDA MEANS *WE'RE* THE ONES BANISHING *OURSELVES...*

WHAT?! I THOUGHT *I* WAS YOUR FRIEND!

UH...YOU *ARE.* I JUST MEANT--

THEN WHAT DO YOU NEED *THEM* FOR?

I JUST THOUGHT THAT MAYBE...

MY FRIENDSHIP ISN'T *ENOUGH?* IS THAT IT?

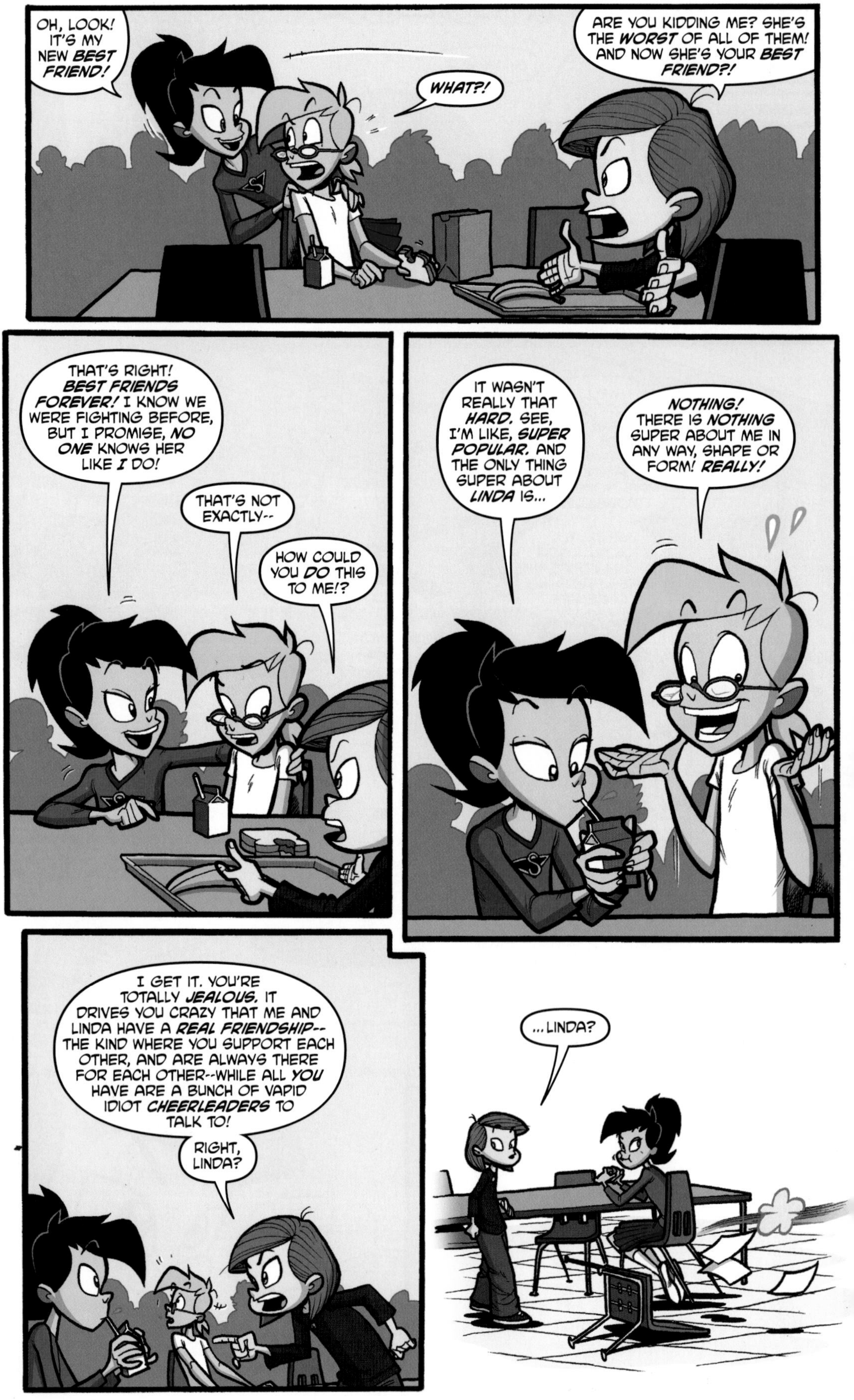
OH, LOOK! IT'S MY NEW BEST FRIEND!
WHAT?!
ARE YOU KIDDING ME? SHE'S THE WORST OF ALL OF THEM! AND NOW SHE'S YOUR BEST FRIEND?!
THAT'S RIGHT! BEST FRIENDS FOREVER! I KNOW WE WERE FIGHTING BEFORE, BUT I PROMISE, NO ONE KNOWS HER LIKE I DO!
THAT'S NOT EXACTLY--
HOW COULD YOU DO THIS TO ME!?
IT WASN'T REALLY THAT HARD. SEE, I'M LIKE, SUPER POPULAR. AND THE ONLY THING SUPER ABOUT LINDA IS...
NOTHING! THERE IS NOTHING SUPER ABOUT ME IN ANY WAY, SHAPE OR FORM! REALLY!
I GET IT. YOU'RE TOTALLY JEALOUS. IT DRIVES YOU CRAZY THAT ME AND LINDA HAVE A REAL FRIENDSHIP-- THE KIND WHERE YOU SUPPORT EACH OTHER, AND ARE ALWAYS THERE FOR EACH OTHER--WHILE ALL YOU HAVE ARE A BUNCH OF VAPID IDIOT CHEERLEADERS TO TALK TO!
RIGHT, LINDA?
...LINDA?

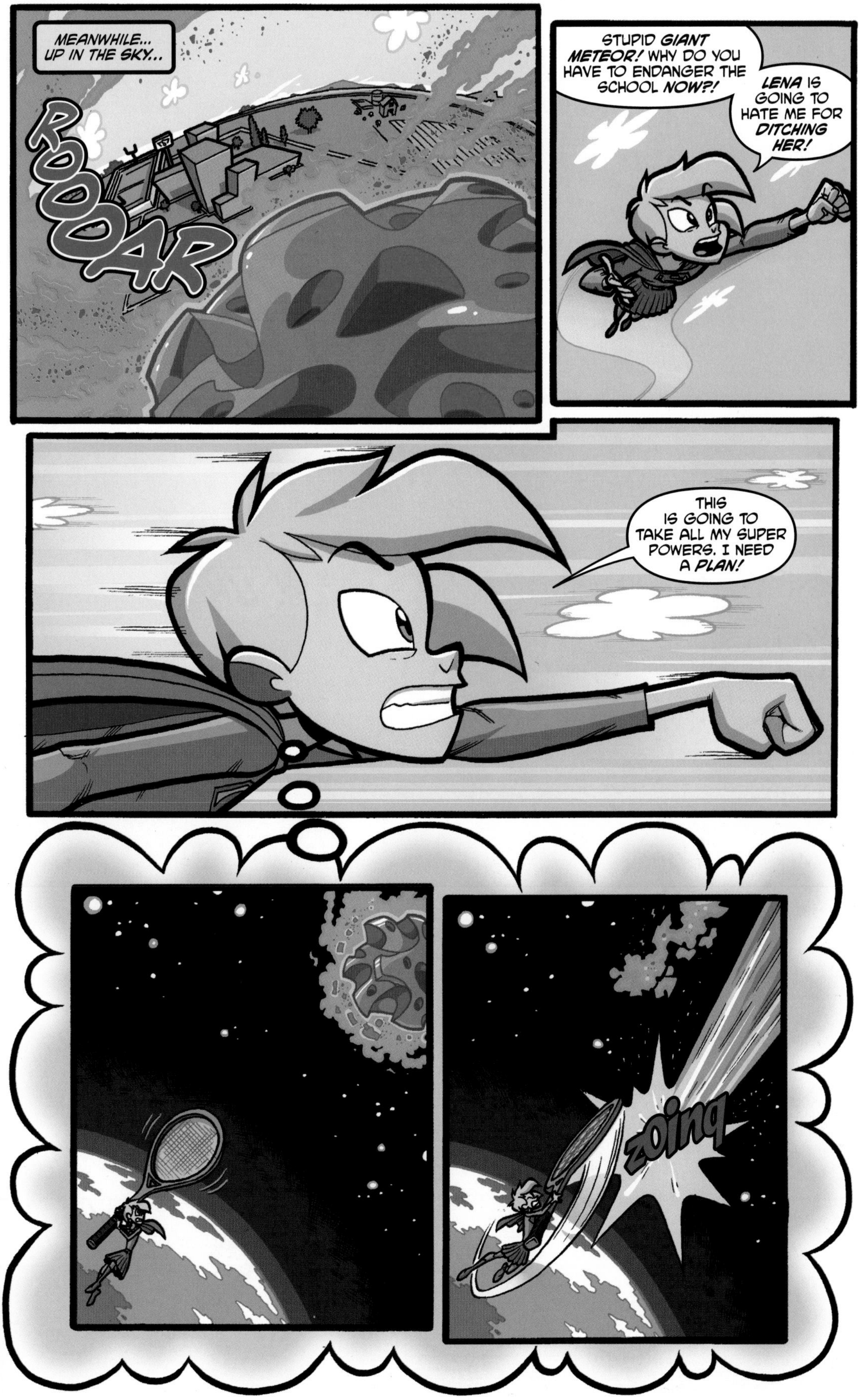
MEANWHILE... UP IN THE SKY...
RODOAR
STUPID GIANT METEOR! WHY DO YOU HAVE TO ENDANGER THE SCHOOL NOW?!
LENA IS GOING TO HATE ME FOR DITCHING HER!
THIS IS GOING TO TAKE ALL MY SUPER POWERS. I NEED A PLAN!
ZOINQ

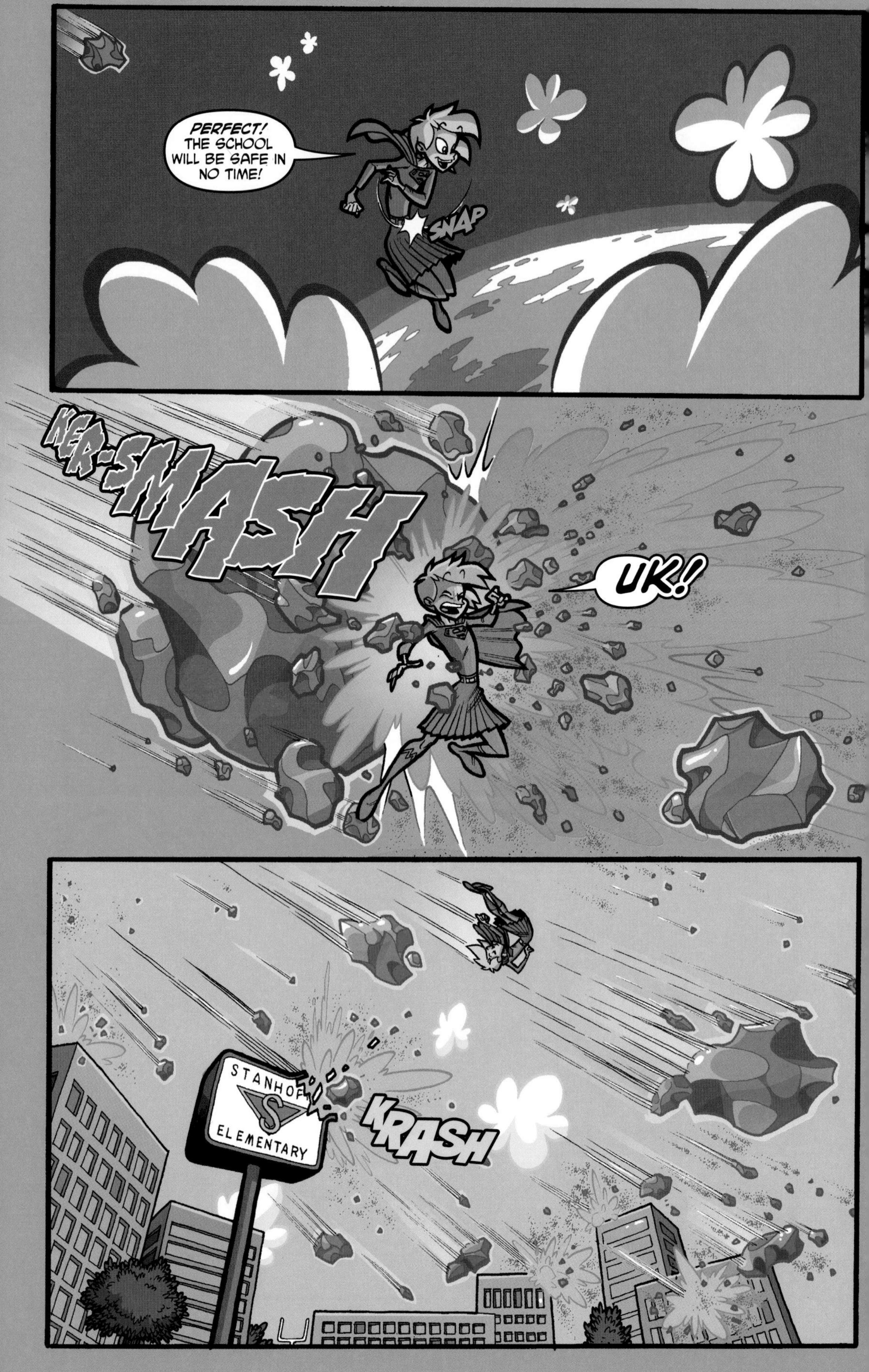
PERFECT! THE SCHOOL WILL BE SAFE IN NO TIME!
SNAP
KER-SMASH
UK!
STANHOPE ELEMENTARY
KRASH

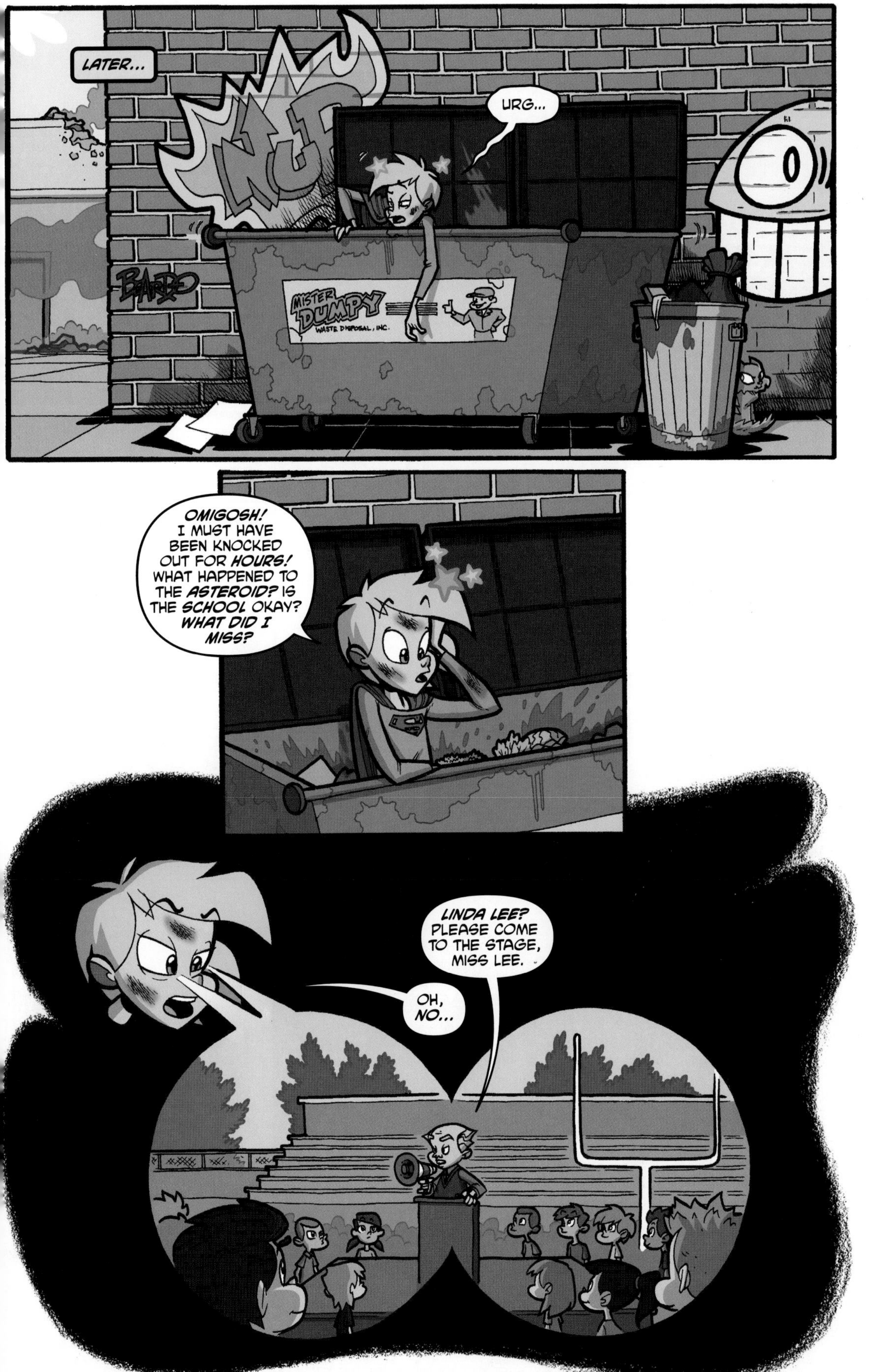
LATER...
URG...
MISTER DUMPY WASTE DISPOSAL, INC.
OMIGOSH! I MUST HAVE BEEN KNOCKED OUT FOR HOURS! WHAT HAPPENED TO THE ASTEROID? IS THE SCHOOL OKAY? WHAT DID I MISS?
LINDA LEE? PLEASE COME TO THE STAGE, MISS LEE.
OH, NO...

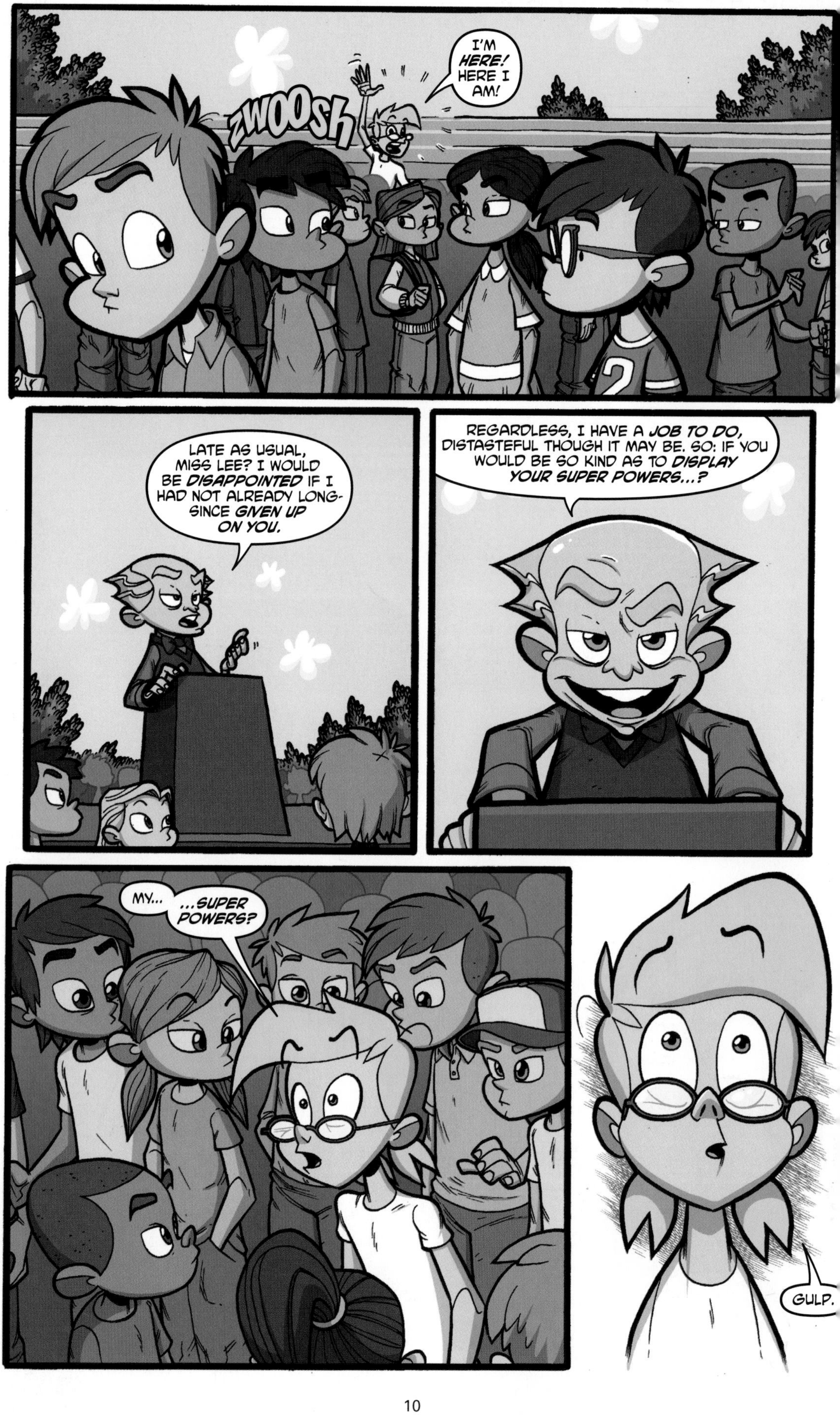

ZWOOSH
I'M HERE! HERE I AM!
LATE AS USUAL, MISS LEE? I WOULD BE DISAPPOINTED IF I HAD NOT ALREADY LONG-SINCE GIVEN UP ON YOU.
REGARDLESS, I HAVE A JOB TO DO, DISTASTEFUL THOUGH IT MAY BE. SO: IF YOU WOULD BE SO KIND AS TO DISPLAY YOUR SUPER POWERS...?
MY...
...SUPER POWERS?
GULP.

PART 2: WITH GREAT POWER...

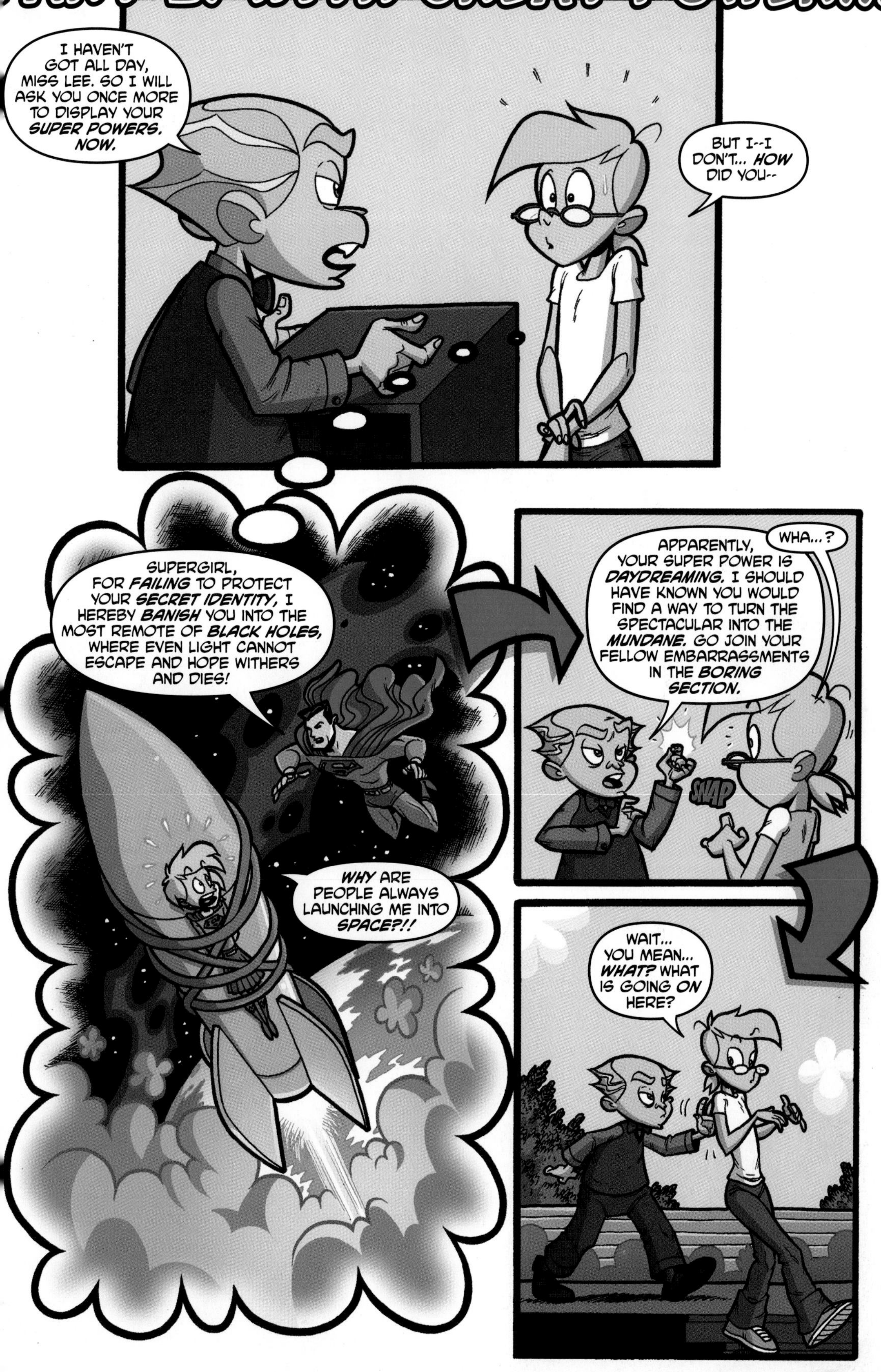

I HAVEN'T GOT ALL DAY, MISS LEE. SO I WILL ASK YOU ONCE MORE TO DISPLAY YOUR SUPER POWERS. NOW.
BUT I--I DON'T... HOW DID YOU--
SUPERGIRL, FOR FAILING TO PROTECT YOUR SECRET IDENTITY, I HEREBY BANISH YOU INTO THE MOST REMOTE OF BLACK HOLES, WHERE EVEN LIGHT CANNOT ESCAPE AND HOPE WITHERS AND DIES!
WHY ARE PEOPLE ALWAYS LAUNCHING ME INTO SPACE?!!
APPARENTLY, YOUR SUPER POWER IS DAYDREAMING. I SHOULD HAVE KNOWN YOU WOULD FIND A WAY TO TURN THE SPECTACULAR INTO THE MUNDANE. GO JOIN YOUR FELLOW EMBARRASSMENTS IN THE BORING SECTION.
WHA...?
SNAP
WAIT... YOU MEAN... WHAT? WHAT IS GOING ON HERE?

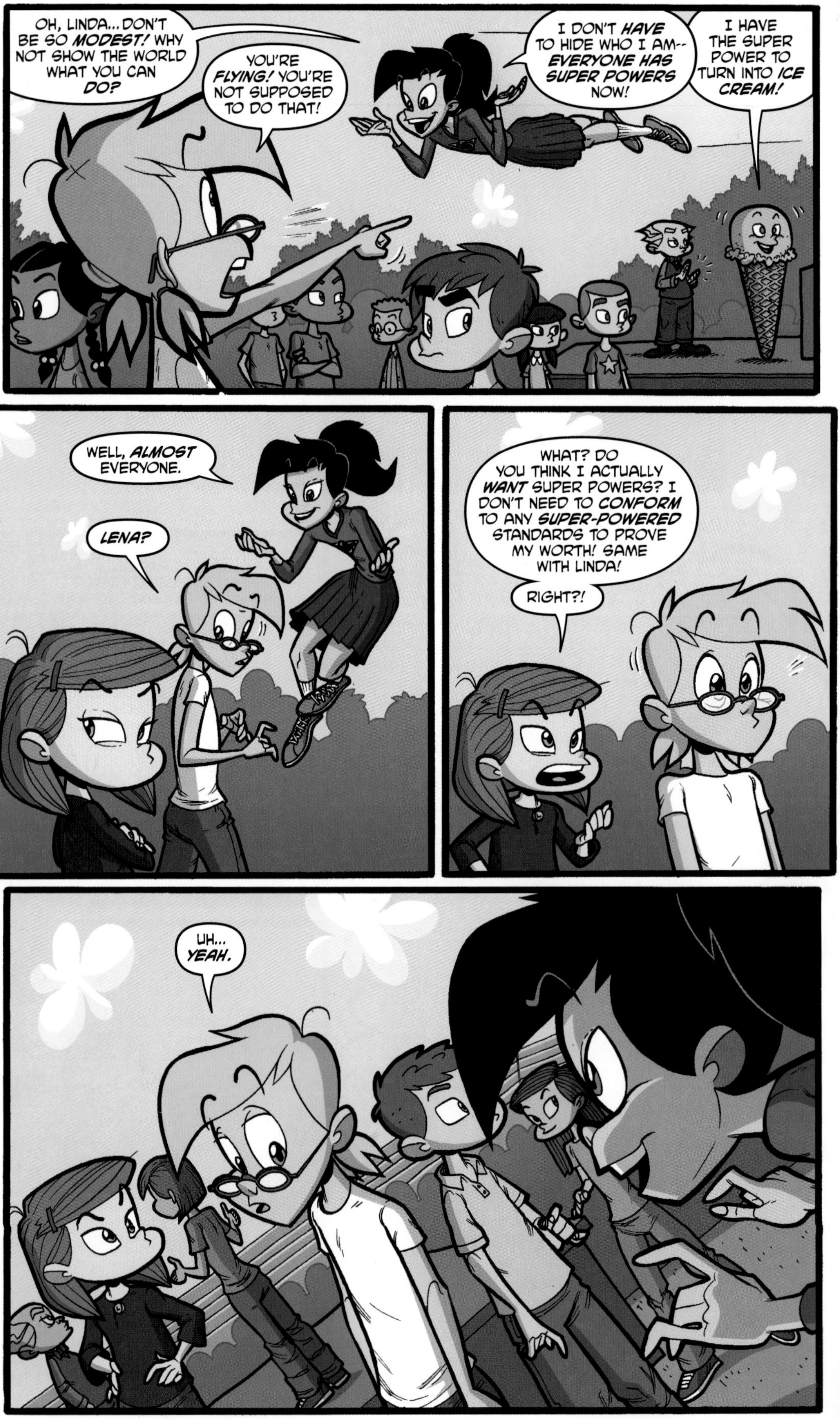

OH, LINDA... DON'T BE SO MODEST! WHY NOT SHOW THE WORLD WHAT YOU CAN DO?
YOU'RE FLYING! YOU'RE NOT SUPPOSED TO DO THAT!
I DON'T HAVE TO HIDE WHO I AM-- EVERYONE HAS SUPER POWERS NOW!
I HAVE THE SUPER POWER TO TURN INTO ICE CREAM!
WELL, ALMOST EVERYONE.
LENA?
WHAT? DO YOU THINK I ACTUALLY WANT SUPER POWERS? I DON'T NEED TO CONFORM TO ANY SUPER-POWERED STANDARDS TO PROVE MY WORTH! SAME WITH LINDA!
RIGHT?!
UH... YEAH.

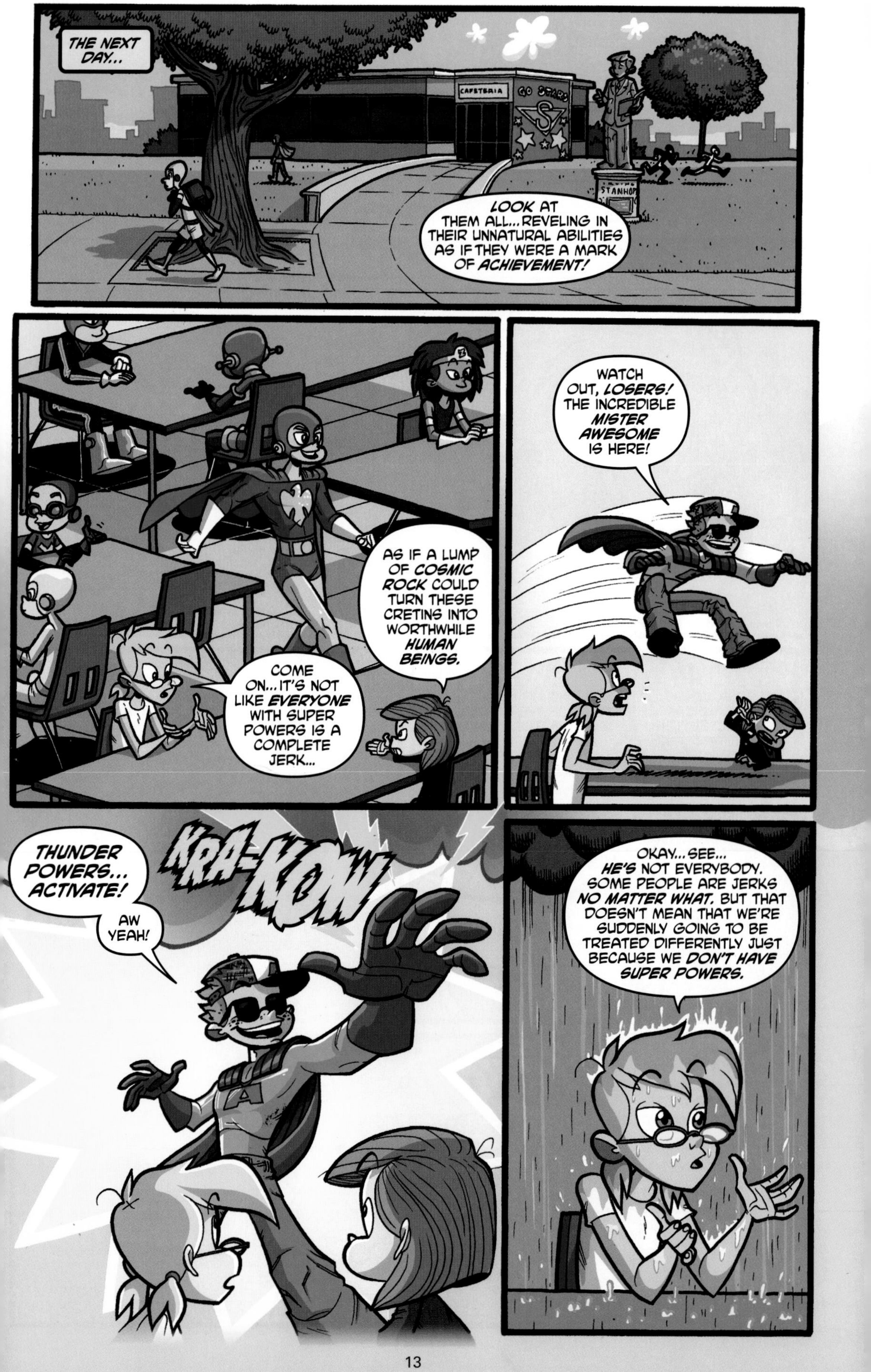
THE NEXT DAY...
CAFETERIA
GO STARS
STANHOPE
LOOK AT THEM ALL... REVELING IN THEIR UNNATURAL ABILITIES AS IF THEY WERE A MARK OF ACHIEVEMENT!
AS IF A LUMP OF COSMIC ROCK COULD TURN THESE CRETINS INTO WORTHWHILE HUMAN BEINGS.
COME ON... IT'S NOT LIKE EVERYONE WITH SUPER POWERS IS A COMPLETE JERK...
WATCH OUT, LOSERS! THE INCREDIBLE MISTER AWESOME IS HERE!
THUNDER POWERS... ACTIVATE!
AW YEAH!
KRA-KOW
OKAY... SEE... HE'S NOT EVERYBODY. SOME PEOPLE ARE JERKS NO MATTER WHAT. BUT THAT DOESN'T MEAN THAT WE'RE SUDDENLY GOING TO BE TREATED DIFFERENTLY JUST BECAUSE WE DON'T HAVE SUPER POWERS.

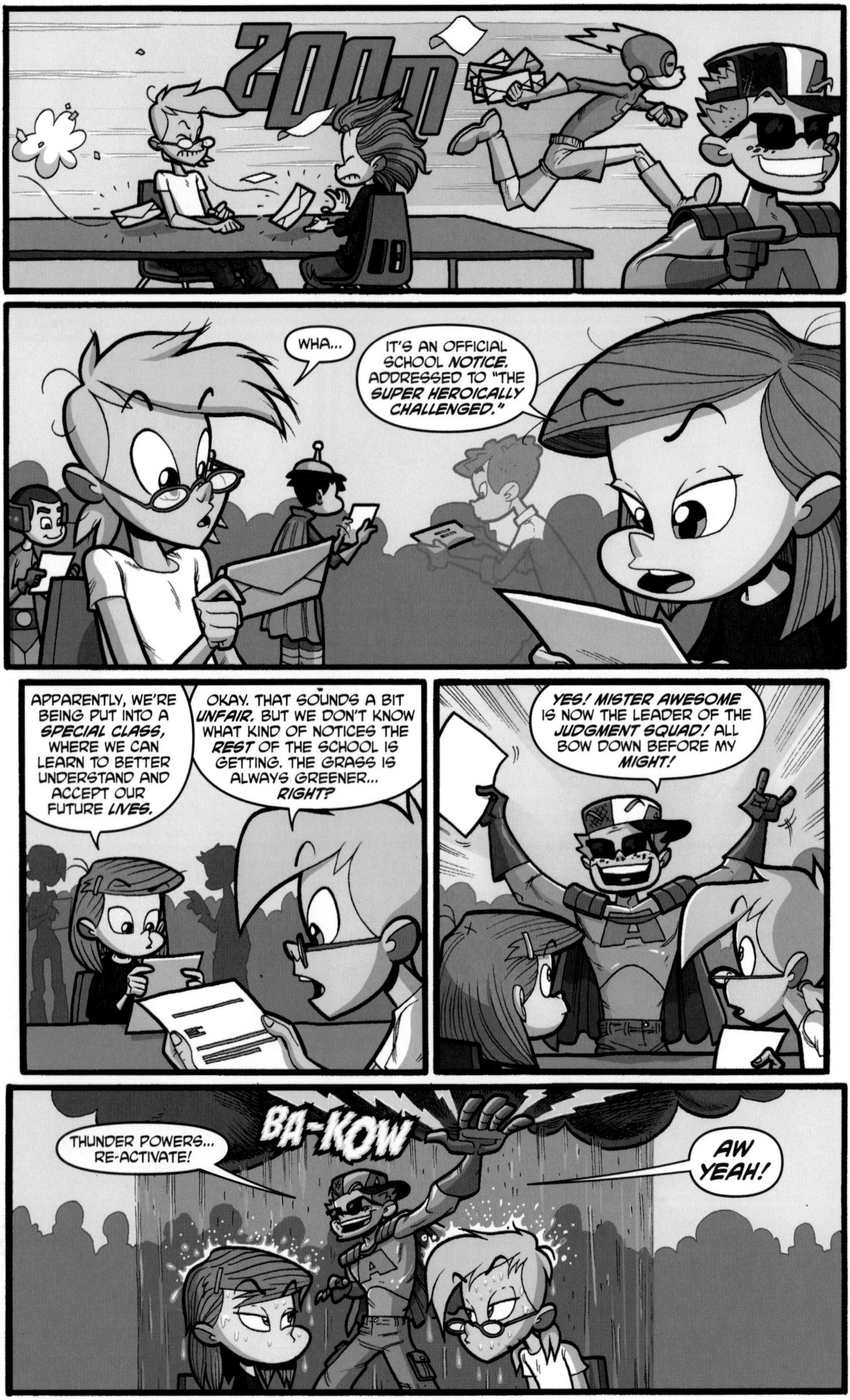
ZOOM
WHA...
IT'S AN OFFICIAL SCHOOL NOTICE. ADDRESSED TO "THE SUPER HEROICALLY CHALLENGED."
APPARENTLY, WE'RE BEING PUT INTO A SPECIAL CLASS, WHERE WE CAN LEARN TO BETTER UNDERSTAND AND ACCEPT OUR FUTURE LIVES.
OKAY. THAT SOUNDS A BIT UNFAIR. BUT WE DON'T KNOW WHAT KIND OF NOTICES THE REST OF THE SCHOOL IS GETTING. THE GRASS IS ALWAYS GREENER... RIGHT?
YES! MISTER AWESOME IS NOW THE LEADER OF THE JUDGMENT SQUAD! ALL BOW DOWN BEFORE MY MIGHT!
BA-KOW
THUNDER POWERS... RE-ACTIVATE!
AW YEAH!

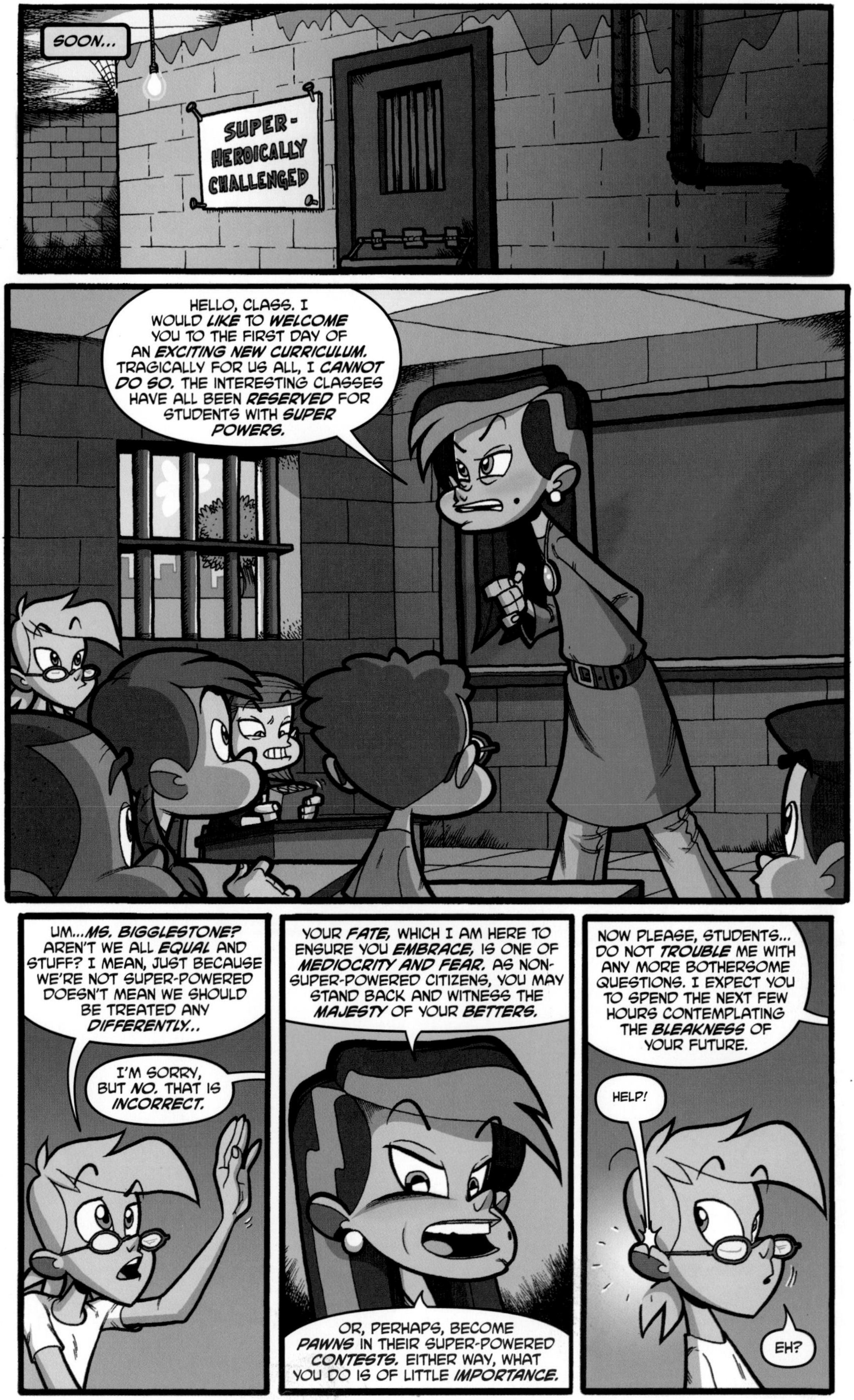
SOON...
SUPER-HEROICALLY CHALLENGED
HELLO, CLASS. I WOULD LIKE TO WELCOME YOU TO THE FIRST DAY OF AN EXCITING NEW CURRICULUM. TRAGICALLY FOR US ALL, I CANNOT DO SO. THE INTERESTING CLASSES HAVE ALL BEEN RESERVED FOR STUDENTS WITH SUPER POWERS.
UM...MS. BIGGLESTONE? AREN'T WE ALL EQUAL AND STUFF? I MEAN, JUST BECAUSE WE'RE NOT SUPER-POWERED DOESN'T MEAN WE SHOULD BE TREATED ANY DIFFERENTLY...
I'M SORRY, BUT NO. THAT IS INCORRECT.
YOUR FATE, WHICH I AM HERE TO ENSURE YOU EMBRACE, IS ONE OF MEDIOCRITY AND FEAR. AS NON-SUPER-POWERED CITIZENS, YOU MAY STAND BACK AND WITNESS THE MAJESTY OF YOUR BETTERS.
OR, PERHAPS, BECOME PAWNS IN THEIR SUPER-POWERED CONTESTS. EITHER WAY, WHAT YOU DO IS OF LITTLE IMPORTANCE.
NOW PLEASE, STUDENTS... DO NOT TROUBLE ME WITH ANY MORE BOTHERSOME QUESTIONS. I EXPECT YOU TO SPEND THE NEXT FEW HOURS CONTEMPLATING THE BLEAKNESS OF YOUR FUTURE.
HELP!
EH?

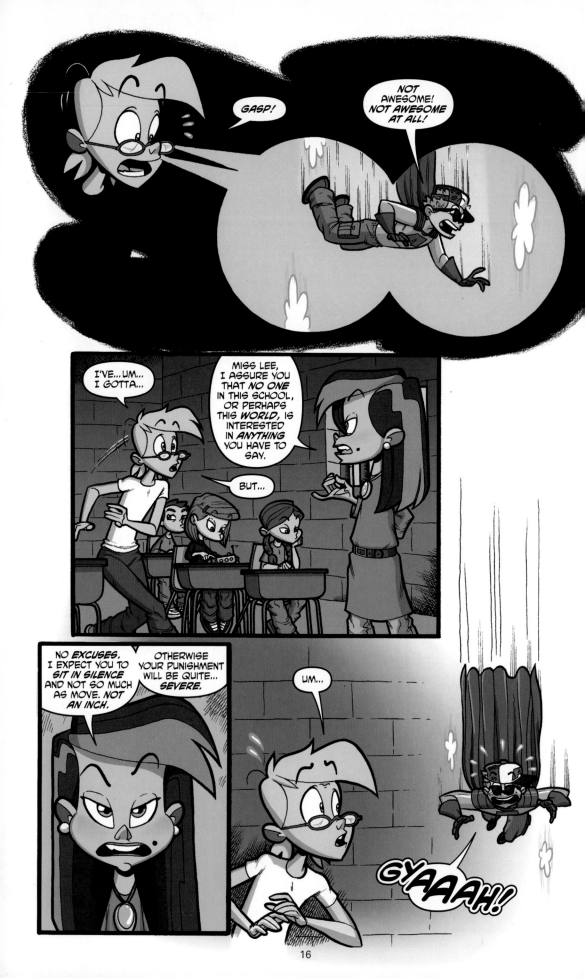

GASP!

NOT AWESOME! NOT AWESOME AT ALL!

I'VE...UM... I GOTTA...

MISS LEE, I ASSURE YOU THAT *NO ONE* IN THIS SCHOOL, OR PERHAPS THIS *WORLD*, IS INTERESTED IN *ANYTHING* YOU HAVE TO SAY.

BUT...

NO *EXCUSES*. I EXPECT YOU TO *SIT IN SILENCE* AND NOT SO MUCH AS MOVE. *NOT AN INCH*.

OTHERWISE YOUR PUNISHMENT WILL BE QUITE... *SEVERE*.

UM...

GYAAAH!

PART 3: POWERLESS!

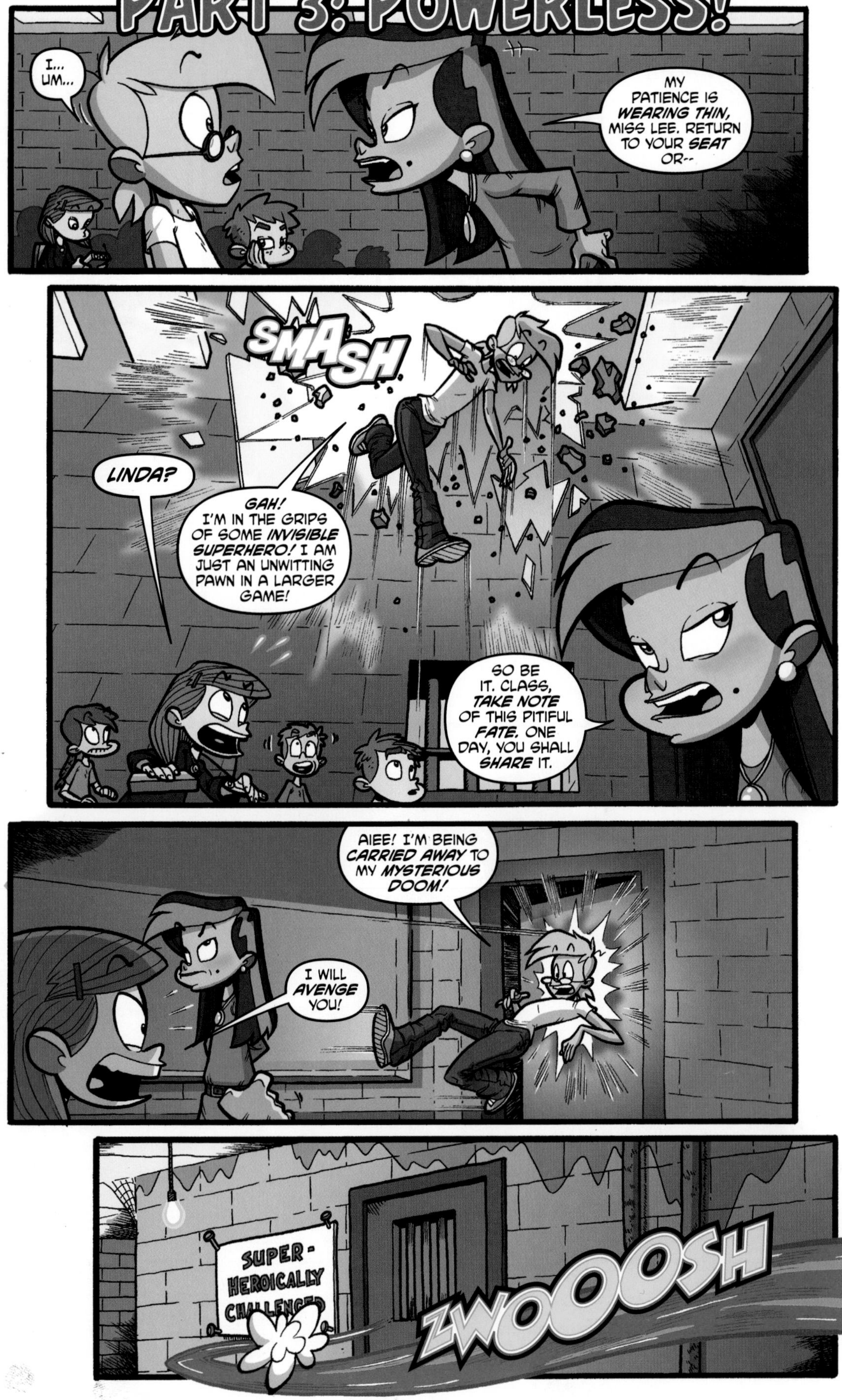

I... UM...
MY PATIENCE IS WEARING THIN, MISS LEE. RETURN TO YOUR SEAT OR--
SMASH
LINDA?
GAH! I'M IN THE GRIPS OF SOME INVISIBLE SUPERHERO! I AM JUST AN UNWITTING PAWN IN A LARGER GAME!
SO BE IT. CLASS, TAKE NOTE OF THIS PITIFUL FATE. ONE DAY, YOU SHALL SHARE IT.
AIEE! I'M BEING CARRIED AWAY TO MY MYSTERIOUS DOOM!
I WILL AVENGE YOU!
SUPER-HEROICALLY CHALLENGED
ZWOOOSH

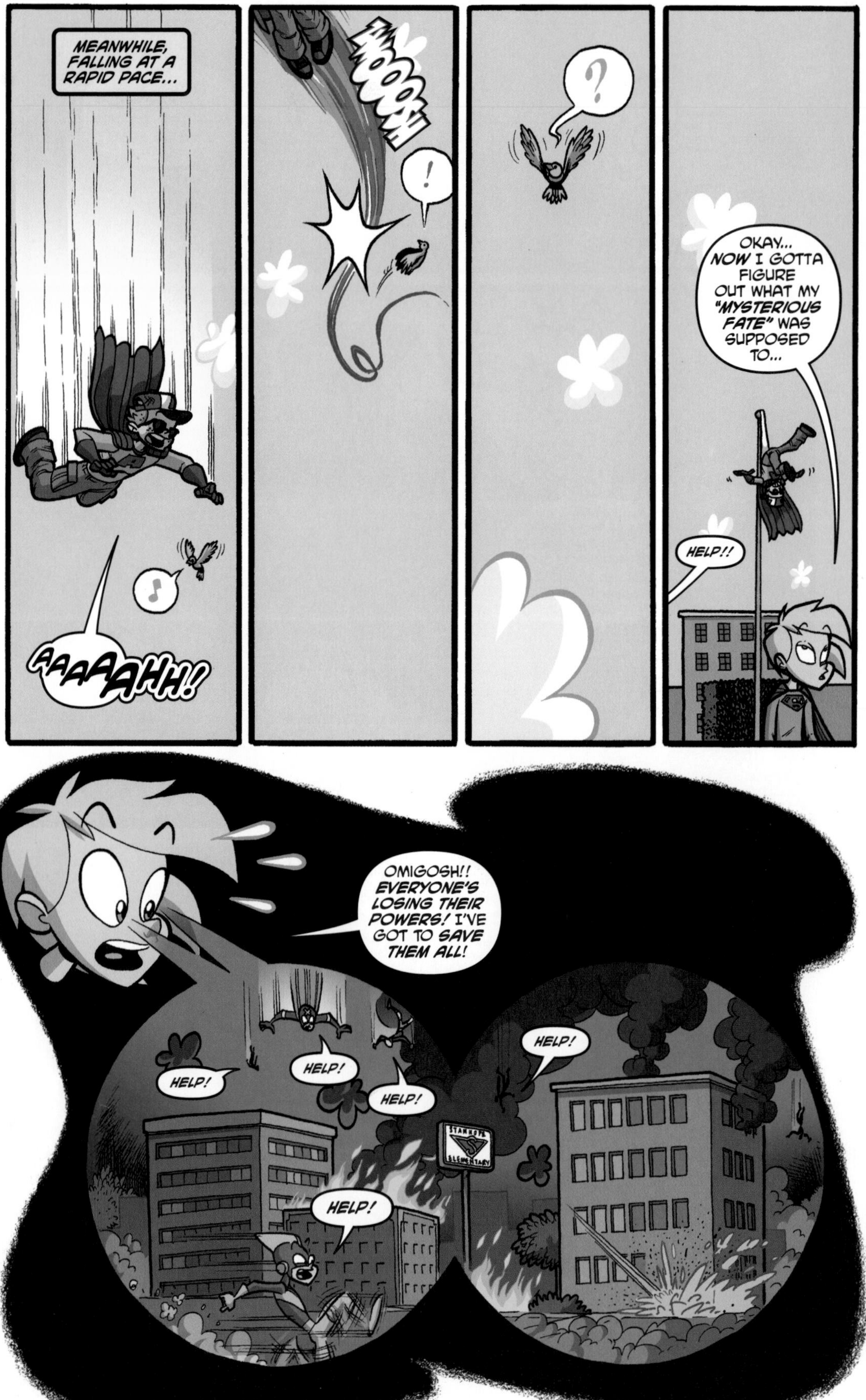

MEANWHILE, FALLING AT A RAPID PACE...
AAAAAHH!
WHOOOOSH
!
?
OKAY... NOW I GOTTA FIGURE OUT WHAT MY "MYSTERIOUS FATE" WAS SUPPOSED TO...
HELP!!
OMIGOSH!! EVERYONE'S LOSING THEIR POWERS! I'VE GOT TO SAVE THEM ALL!
HELP!
HELP!
HELP!
HELP!
HELP!

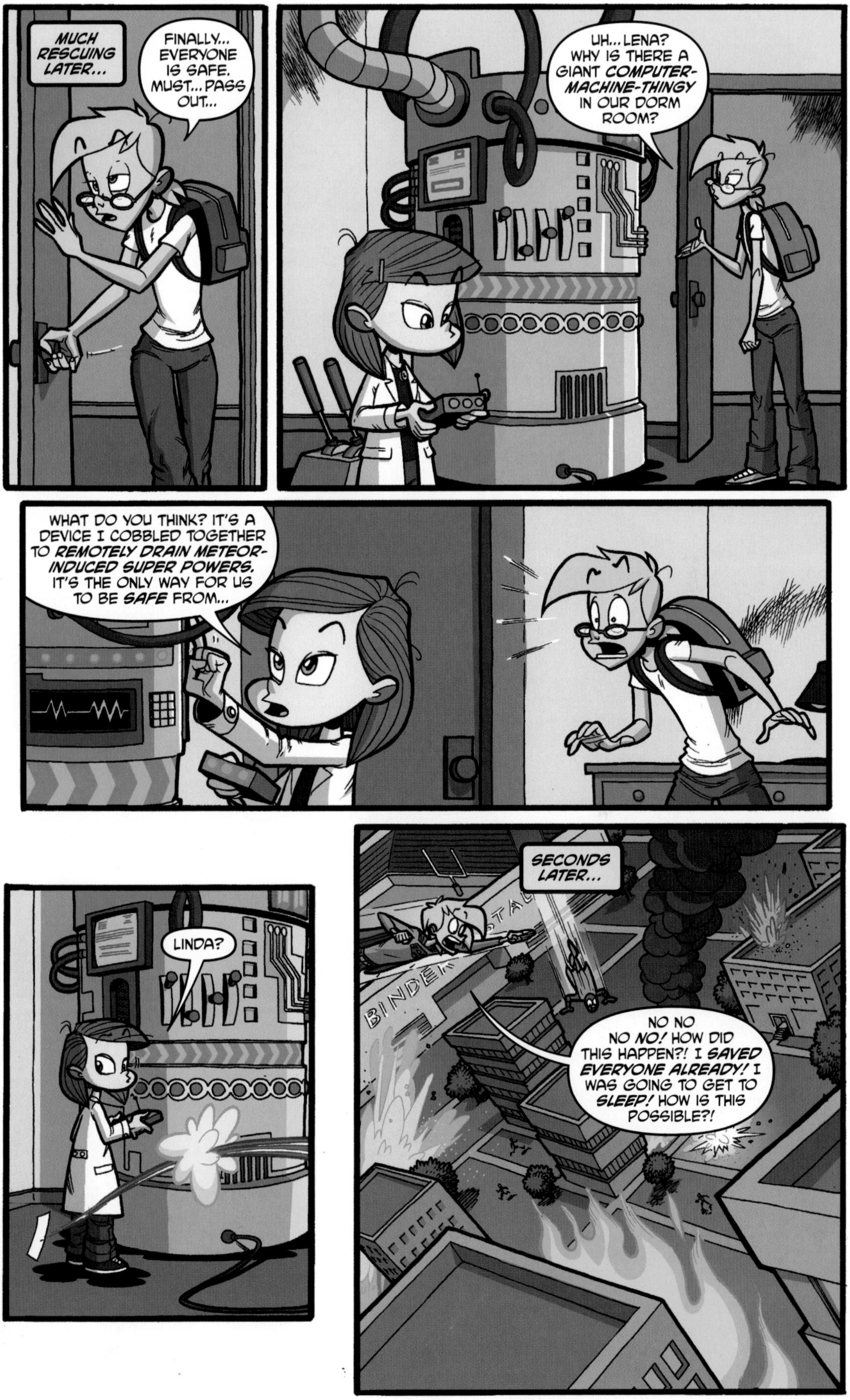
MUCH RESCUING LATER...
FINALLY... EVERYONE IS SAFE. MUST...PASS OUT...
UH... LENA? WHY IS THERE A GIANT COMPUTER-MACHINE-THINGY IN OUR DORM ROOM?
WHAT DO YOU THINK? IT'S A DEVICE I COBBLED TOGETHER TO REMOTELY DRAIN METEOR-INDUCED SUPER POWERS. IT'S THE ONLY WAY FOR US TO BE SAFE FROM...
LINDA?
SECONDS LATER...
BINDER
NO NO NO NO! HOW DID THIS HAPPEN?! I SAVED EVERYONE ALREADY! I WAS GOING TO GET TO SLEEP! HOW IS THIS POSSIBLE?!

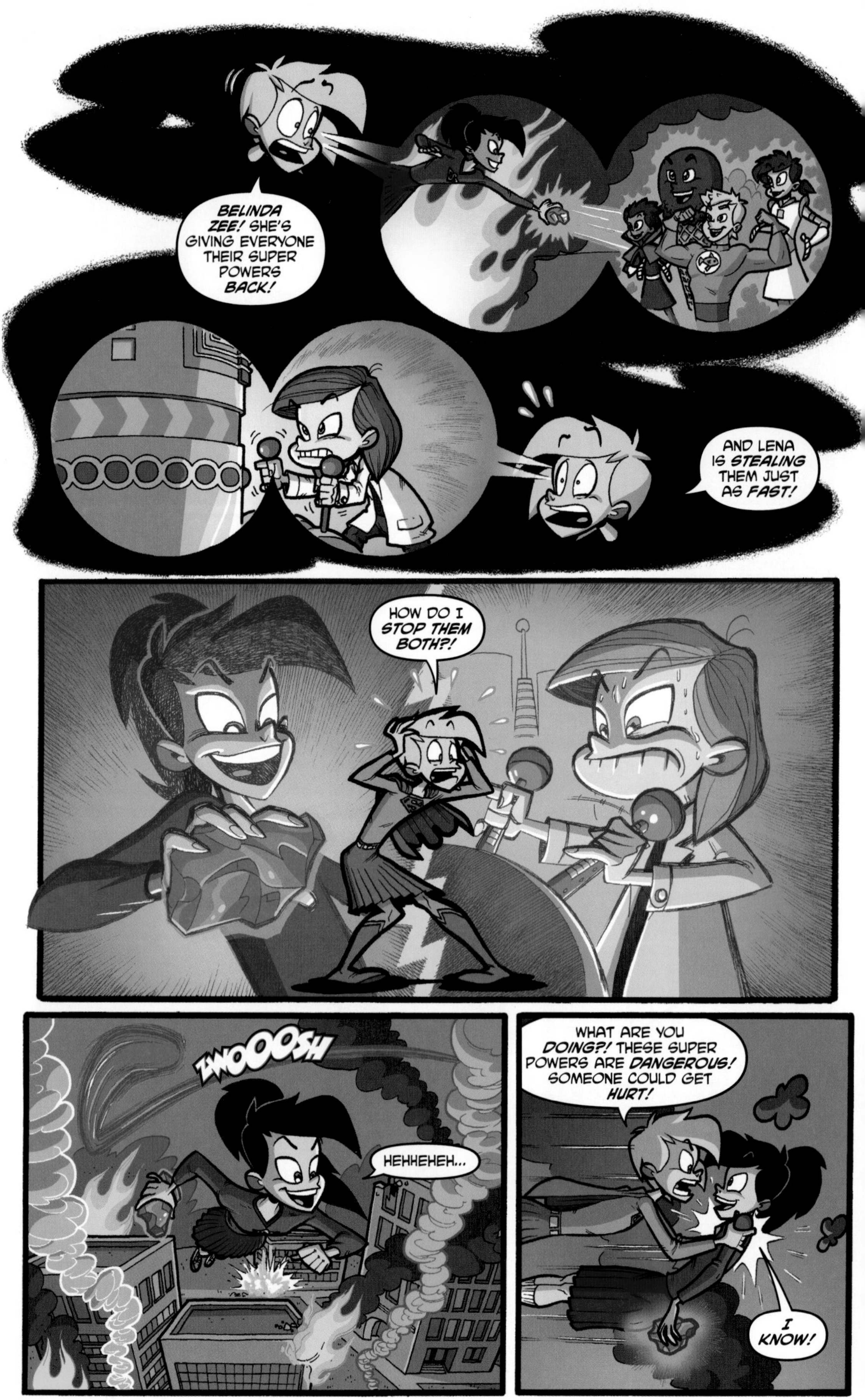
BELINDA ZEE! SHE'S GIVING EVERYONE THEIR SUPER POWERS BACK!
AND LENA IS STEALING THEM JUST AS FAST!
HOW DO I STOP THEM BOTH?!
ZWOOOSH
HEHHEHEH...
WHAT ARE YOU DOING?! THESE SUPER POWERS ARE DANGEROUS! SOMEONE COULD GET HURT!
I KNOW!

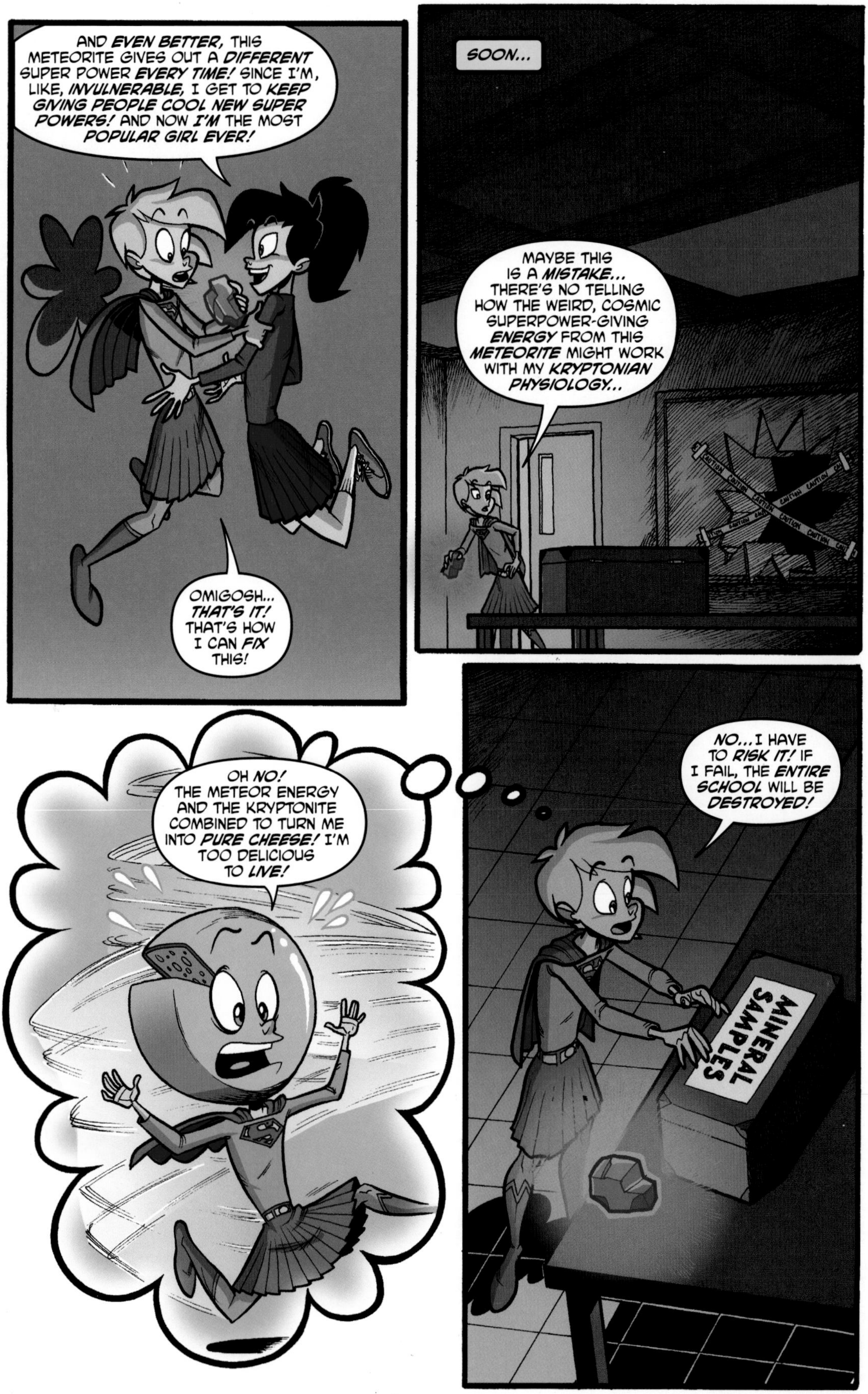

AND EVEN BETTER, THIS METEORITE GIVES OUT A DIFFERENT SUPER POWER EVERY TIME! SINCE I'M, LIKE, INVULNERABLE, I GET TO KEEP GIVING PEOPLE COOL NEW SUPER POWERS! AND NOW I'M THE MOST POPULAR GIRL EVER!
OMIGOSH... THAT'S IT! THAT'S HOW I CAN FIX THIS!
SOON...
MAYBE THIS IS A MISTAKE... THERE'S NO TELLING HOW THE WEIRD, COSMIC SUPERPOWER-GIVING ENERGY FROM THIS METEORITE MIGHT WORK WITH MY KRYPTONIAN PHYSIOLOGY...
OH NO! THE METEOR ENERGY AND THE KRYPTONITE COMBINED TO TURN ME INTO PURE CHEESE! I'M TOO DELICIOUS TO LIVE!
NO...I HAVE TO RISK IT! IF I FAIL, THE ENTIRE SCHOOL WILL BE DESTROYED!
MINERAL SAMPLES

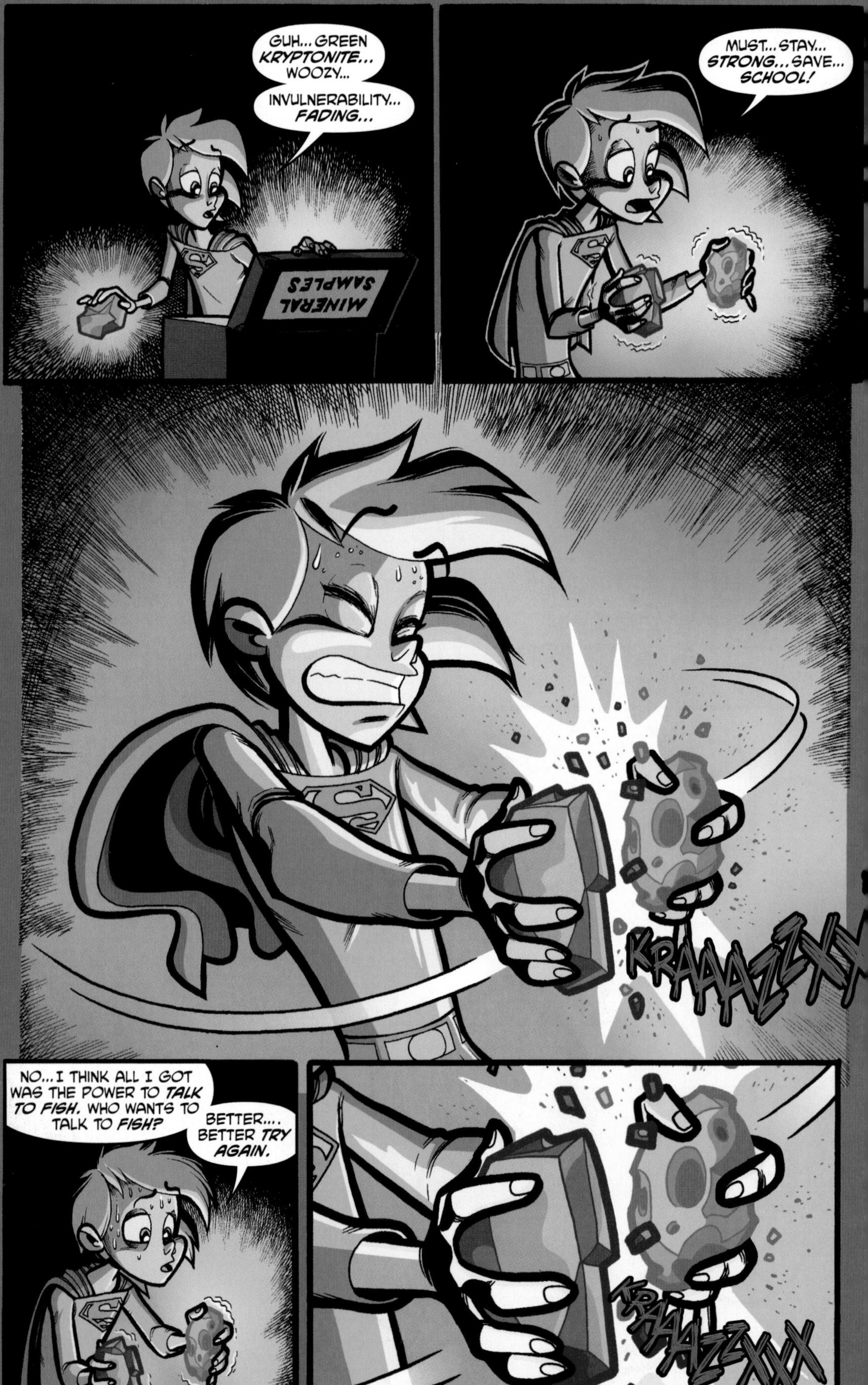
GUH... GREEN KRYPTONITE... WOOZY...
INVULNERABILITY... FADING...
MINERAL SAMPLES
MUST... STAY... STRONG... SAVE... SCHOOL!
KRAAAAZZXX
NO... I THINK ALL I GOT WAS THE POWER TO TALK TO FISH. WHO WANTS TO TALK TO FISH?
BETTER.... BETTER TRY AGAIN.
KRAAAAZZXXX

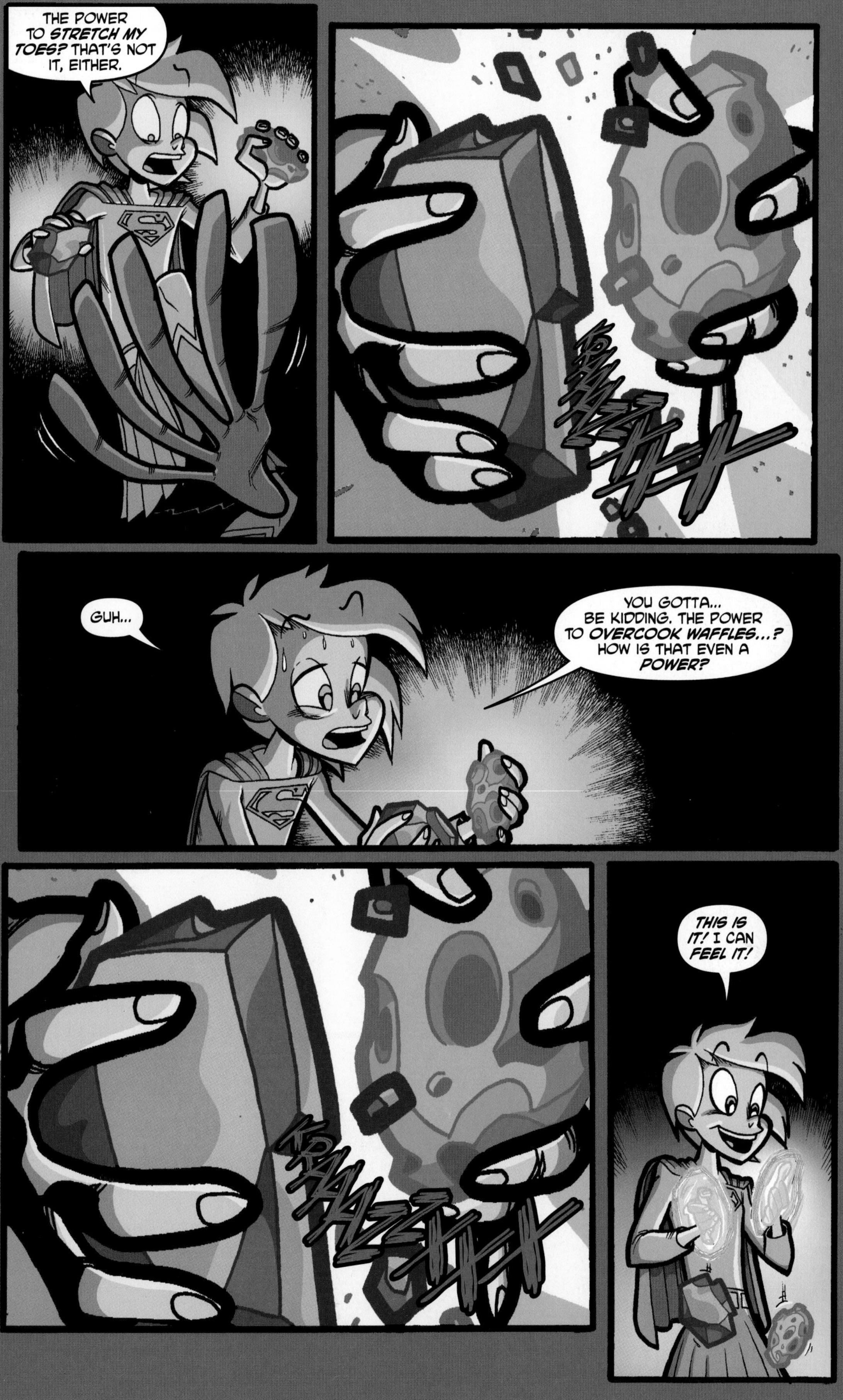
THE POWER TO *STRETCH MY TOES?* THAT'S NOT IT, EITHER.
KRAKAZZ-TH
GUH...
YOU GOTTA... BE KIDDING. THE POWER TO *OVERCOOK WAFFLES...?* HOW IS THAT EVEN A *POWER?*
KRAKAZZ-TH
THIS IS IT! I CAN *FEEL IT!*

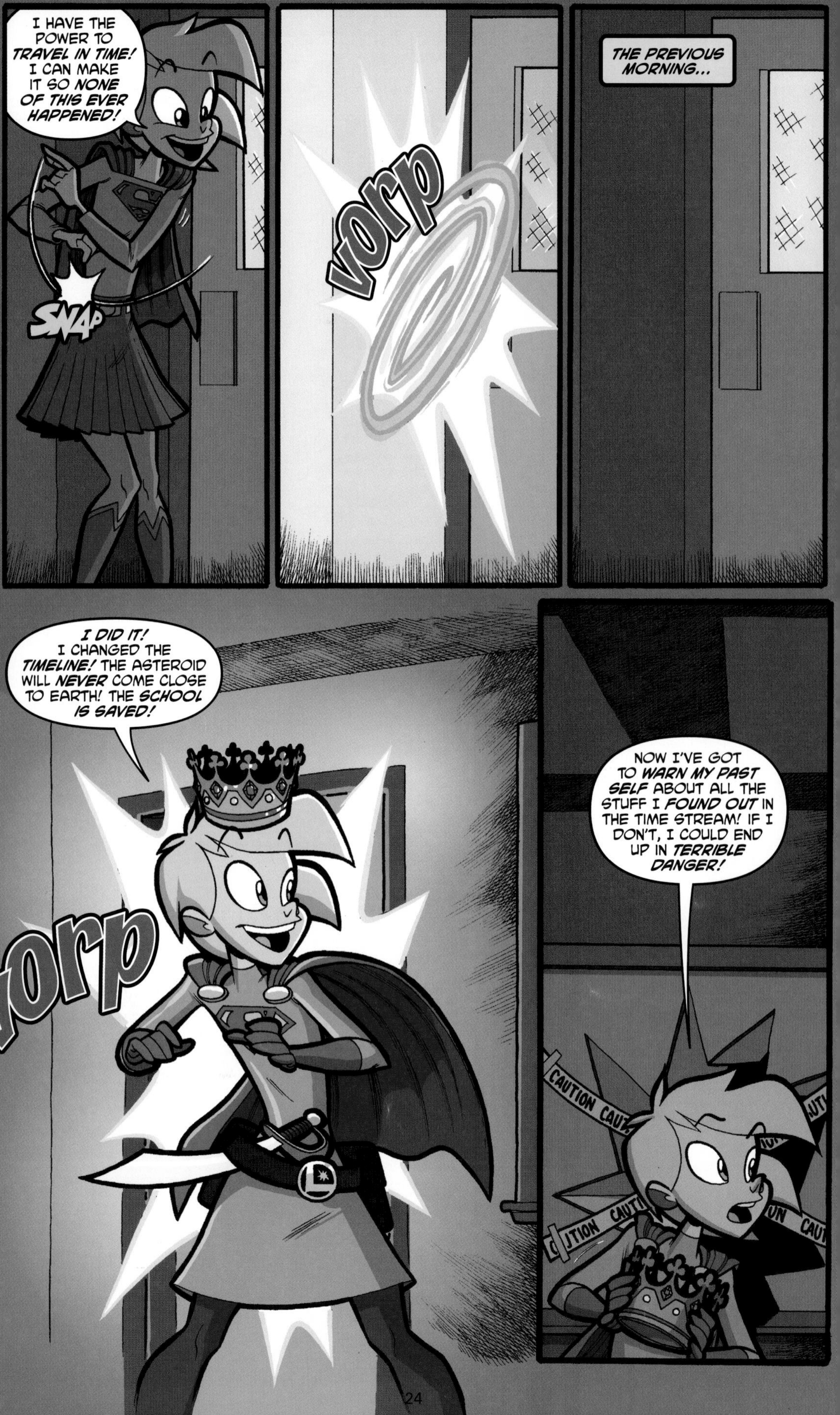
I HAVE THE POWER TO TRAVEL IN TIME! I CAN MAKE IT SO NONE OF THIS EVER HAPPENED!
SNAP
VORP
THE PREVIOUS MORNING...
I DID IT! I CHANGED THE TIMELINE! THE ASTEROID WILL NEVER COME CLOSE TO EARTH! THE SCHOOL IS SAVED!
VORP
NOW I'VE GOT TO WARN MY PAST SELF ABOUT ALL THE STUFF I FOUND OUT IN THE TIME STREAM! IF I DON'T, I COULD END UP IN TERRIBLE DANGER!
CAUTION CAUT
CAUTION CAUTI

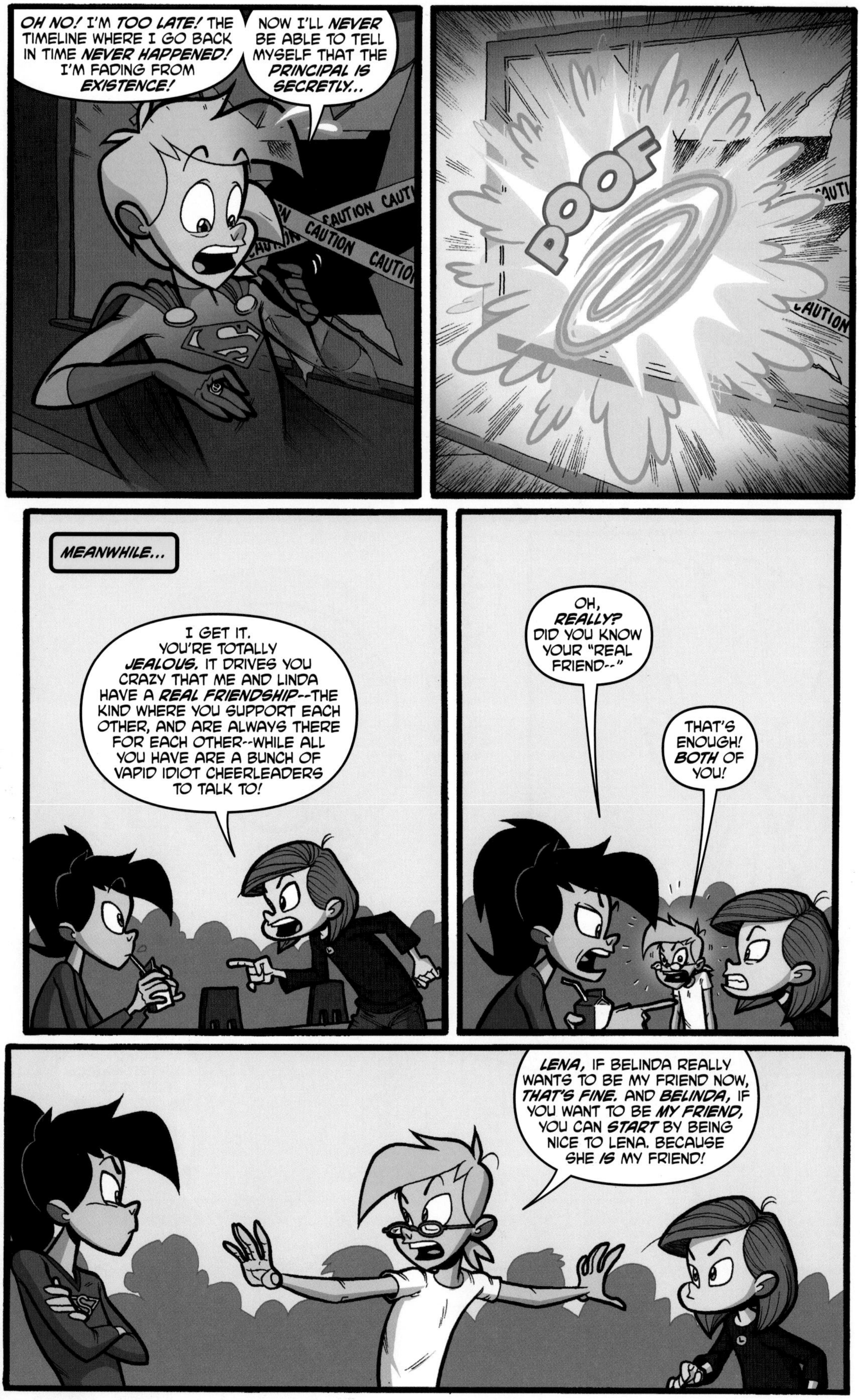
OH NO! I'M TOO LATE! THE TIMELINE WHERE I GO BACK IN TIME NEVER HAPPENED! I'M FADING FROM EXISTENCE!
NOW I'LL NEVER BE ABLE TO TELL MYSELF THAT THE PRINCIPAL IS SECRETLY...
CAUTION CAUTION
CAUTION
CAUTION
POOF
CAUTI
CAUTION
MEANWHILE...
I GET IT. YOU'RE TOTALLY JEALOUS. IT DRIVES YOU CRAZY THAT ME AND LINDA HAVE A REAL FRIENDSHIP--THE KIND WHERE YOU SUPPORT EACH OTHER, AND ARE ALWAYS THERE FOR EACH OTHER--WHILE ALL YOU HAVE ARE A BUNCH OF VAPID IDIOT CHEERLEADERS TO TALK TO!
OH, REALLY? DID YOU KNOW YOUR "REAL FRIEND--"
THAT'S ENOUGH! BOTH OF YOU!
LENA, IF BELINDA REALLY WANTS TO BE MY FRIEND NOW, THAT'S FINE. AND BELINDA, IF YOU WANT TO BE MY FRIEND, YOU CAN START BY BEING NICE TO LENA. BECAUSE SHE IS MY FRIEND!

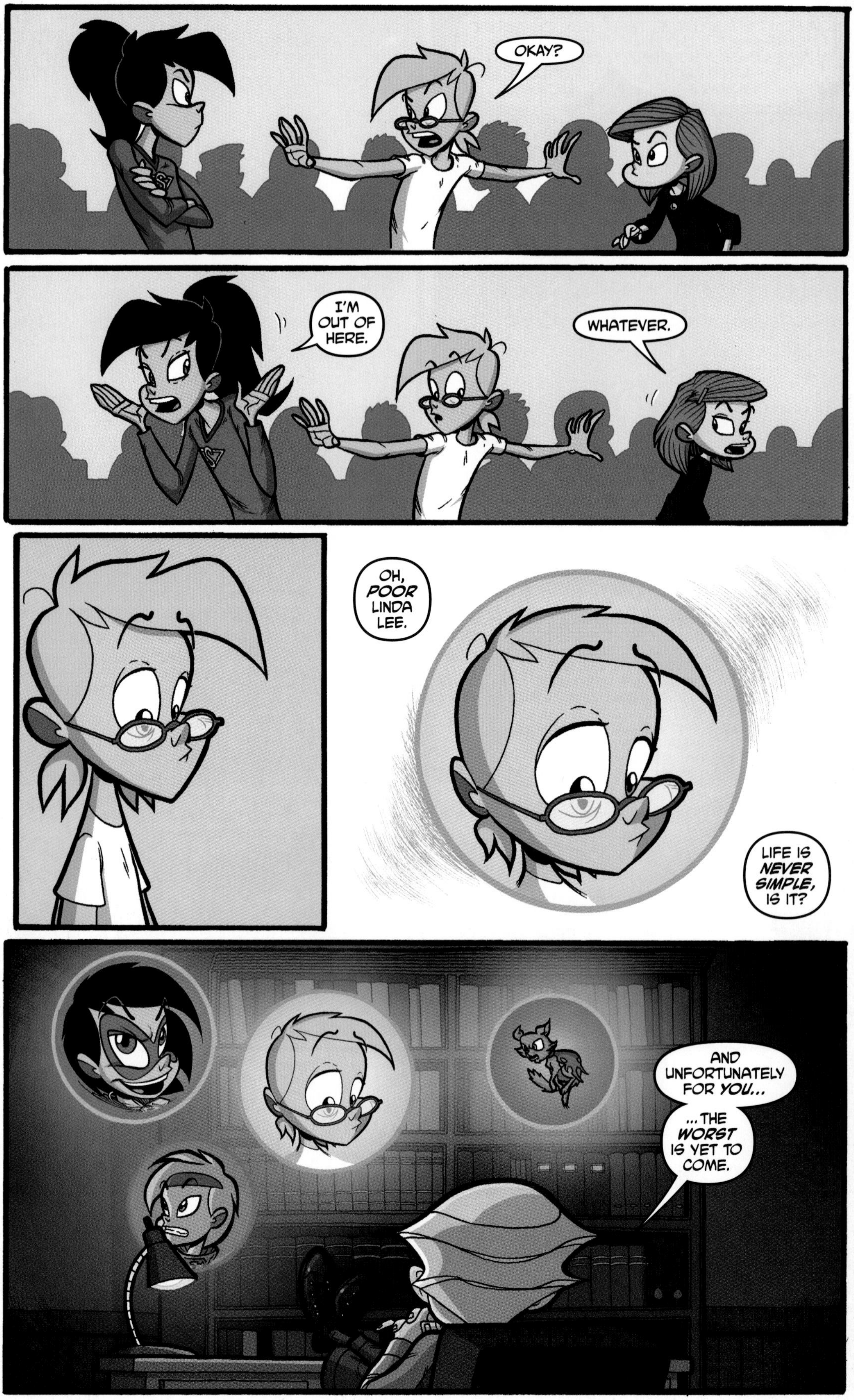
OKAY?
I'M OUT OF HERE.
WHATEVER.
OH, POOR LINDA LEE.
LIFE IS NEVER SIMPLE, IS IT?
AND UNFORTUNATELY FOR YOU...
...THE WORST IS YET TO COME.

CREATORS

LANDRY Q. WALKER WRITER

Landry Q. Walker is a comics writer whose projects include *Supergirl: Cosmic Adventures in the 8th Grade* and more. He has also written *Batman: The Brave and the Bold*, the comic book adventures of The Incredibles, and contributed stories to *Disney Adventures* magazine and the gaming website Elder-Geek.

ERIC JONES ARTIST

Eric Jones is a professional comic book artist whose work for DC Comics includes *Batman: The Brave and the Bold*, *Supergirl: Cosmic Adventures in the 8th Grade*, *Cartoon Network Action Pack*, and more.

JOEY MASON COLORIST

Joey Mason is an illustrator, animation artist, and comic book colorist. His work for DC Comics includes *Supergirl: Cosmic Adventures in the 8th Grade*, as well as set designs for *Green Lantern: The Animated Series*.

GLOSSARY

asteroid [ASS-tur-roid]—a very small planetoid that travels around the sun

avenge [uh-VENJ]—to punish someone for an action or on behalf of a person

banished [BAN-ishd]—sent someone away and ordered the person not to return

cretin [KREE-tin]—an insult meaning an ignorant, lowly person

curriculum [kuh-RIK-you-luhm]—a program of study for a school

mediocrity [mee-dee-AHK-rih-tee]—the quality or state of being average or boring

meteorite [MEE-tee-ur-rite]—a remaining part of a piece of rock or metal that falls to Earth from space before it has burned up

modest [MOD-ist]—not boastful about one's abilities, possessions, or achievements

mundane [muhn-DAYN]—boring and ordinary

pawns [PAWNZ]—people or things that are used to get something or gain an advantage

reveling [REV-uhl-ing]—enjoying something very much

VISUAL QUESTIONS & PROMPTS

1. In this story, the students of Stanhope Boarding School get extraordinary powers. If you could have any superpower, what would it be and why?

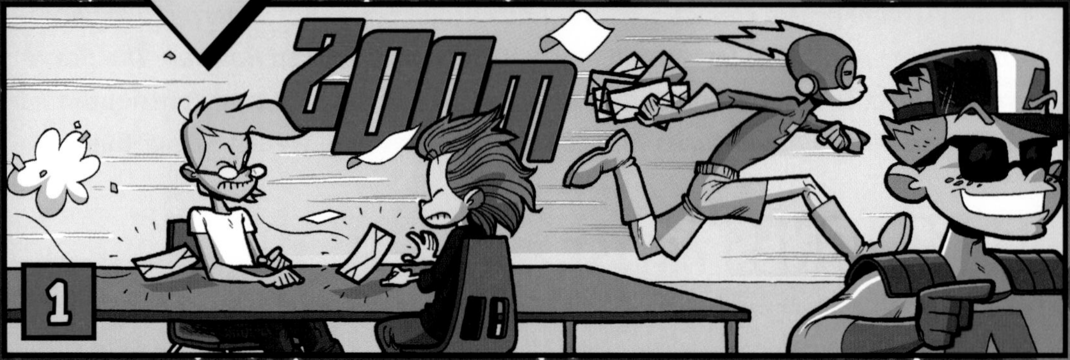
ZOOM
1

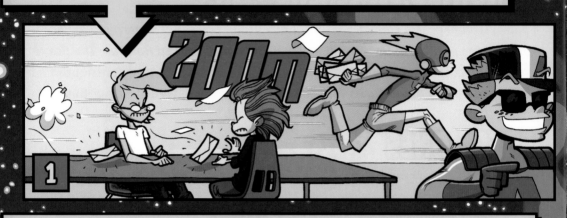

2. In comic books, action often happens in the space between panels. Study the four panels below from page 18. Then describe what is happening between each panel. What clues helped you follow the story from one panel to the next?

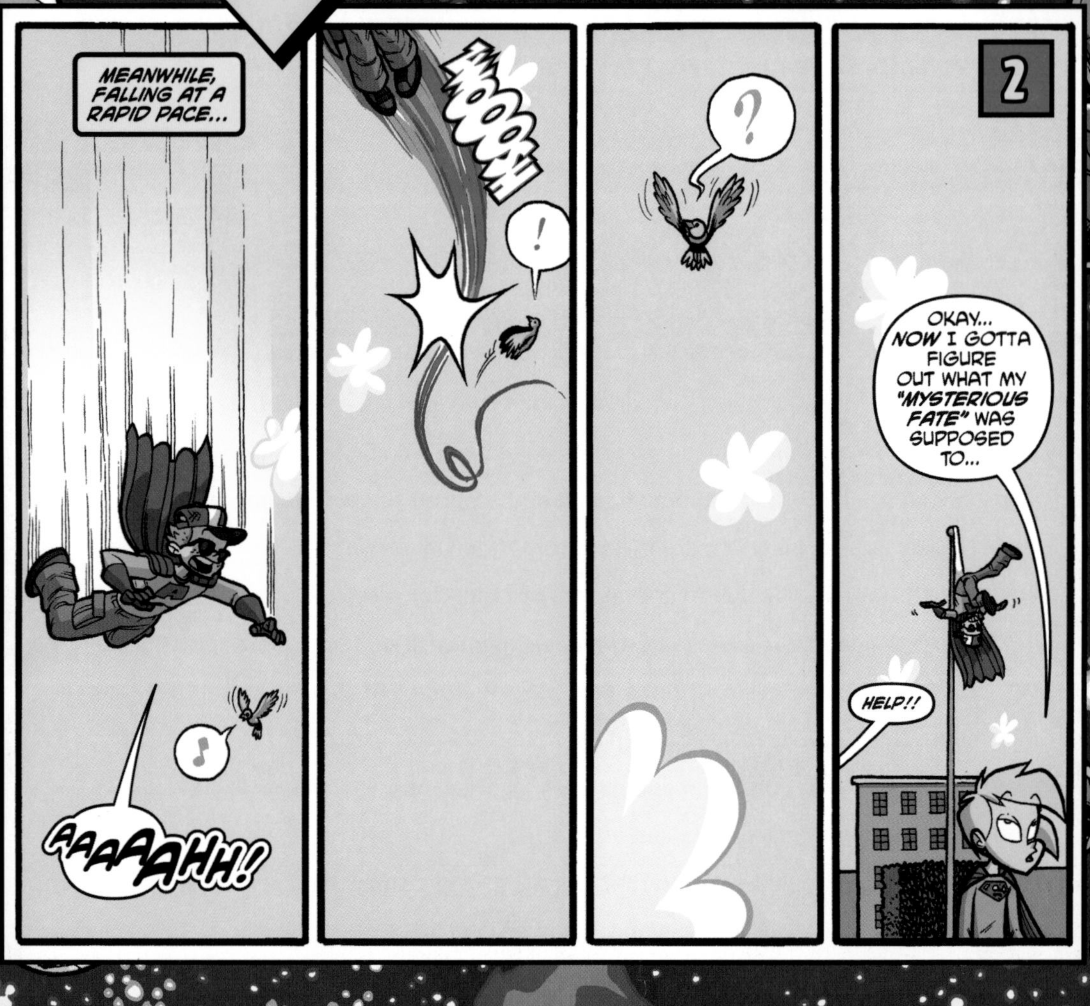
MEANWHILE, FALLING AT A RAPID PACE...
AAAAAHH!
!
?
2
OKAY... NOW I GOTTA FIGURE OUT WHAT MY "MYSTERIOUS FATE" WAS SUPPOSED TO...
HELP!!

3. Study the two panels at right (from page 6). What happens to Linda in the second panel? Explain how you reached your conclusion.

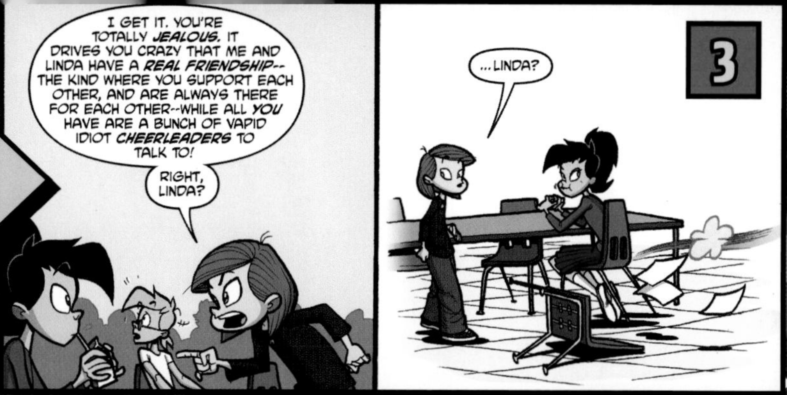
I GET IT. YOU'RE TOTALLY JEALOUS. IT DRIVES YOU CRAZY THAT ME AND LINDA HAVE A REAL FRIENDSHIP-- THE KIND WHERE YOU SUPPORT EACH OTHER, AND ARE ALWAYS THERE FOR EACH OTHER--WHILE ALL YOU HAVE ARE A BUNCH OF VAPID IDIOT CHEERLEADERS TO TALK TO!
RIGHT, LINDA?
...LINDA?
3

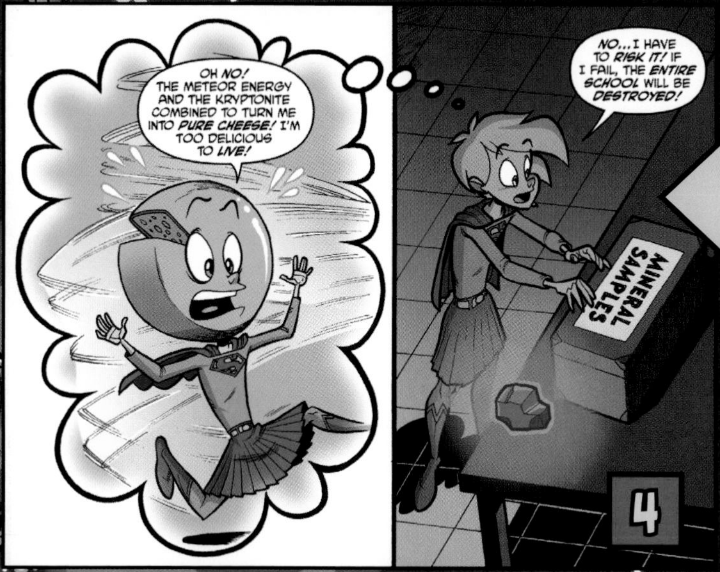
OH NO! THE METEOR ENERGY AND THE KRYPTONITE COMBINED TO TURN ME INTO PURE CHEESE! I'M TOO DELICIOUS TO LIVE!
NO...I HAVE TO RISK IT! IF I FAIL, THE ENTIRE SCHOOL WILL BE DESTROYED!
MINERAL SAMPLES
4

4. Throughout the story, the artist illustrates Supergirl's thoughts with comic book elements called "thought bubbles." Describe another way you could show or tell what a character is thinking.

5. In the final panel, several images foreshadow what's to come in the next story. Why is Belinda wearing a mask? What is Streaky the Super-Cat doing? Write down what you think will happen. Then read the next story and find out if you're right!

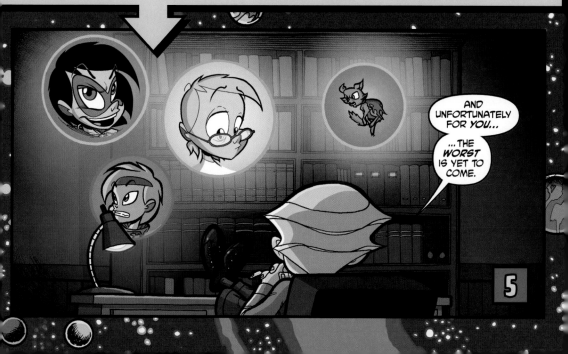

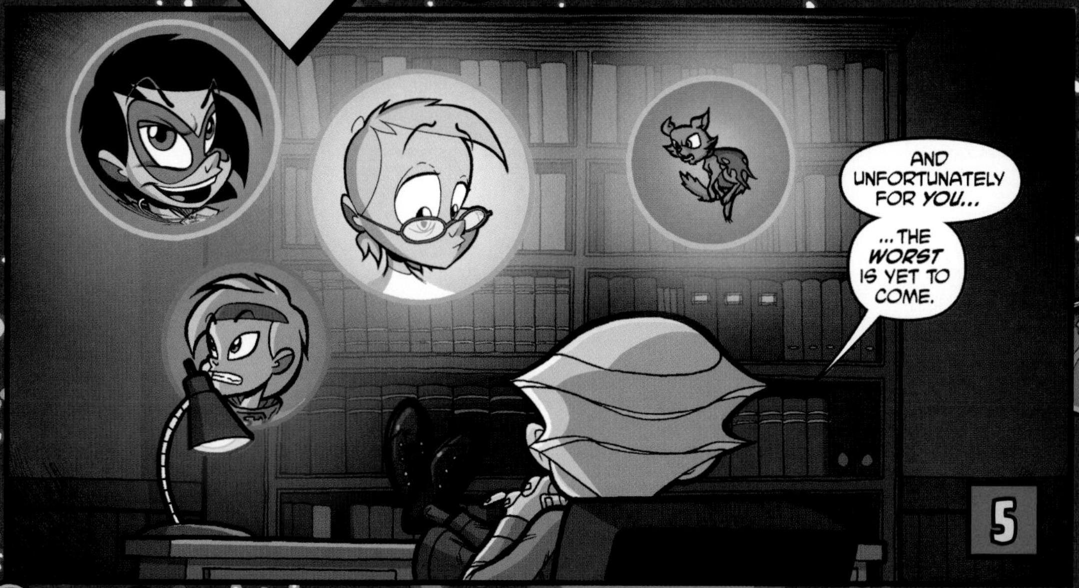
AND UNFORTUNATELY FOR YOU...
...THE WORST IS YET TO COME.
5

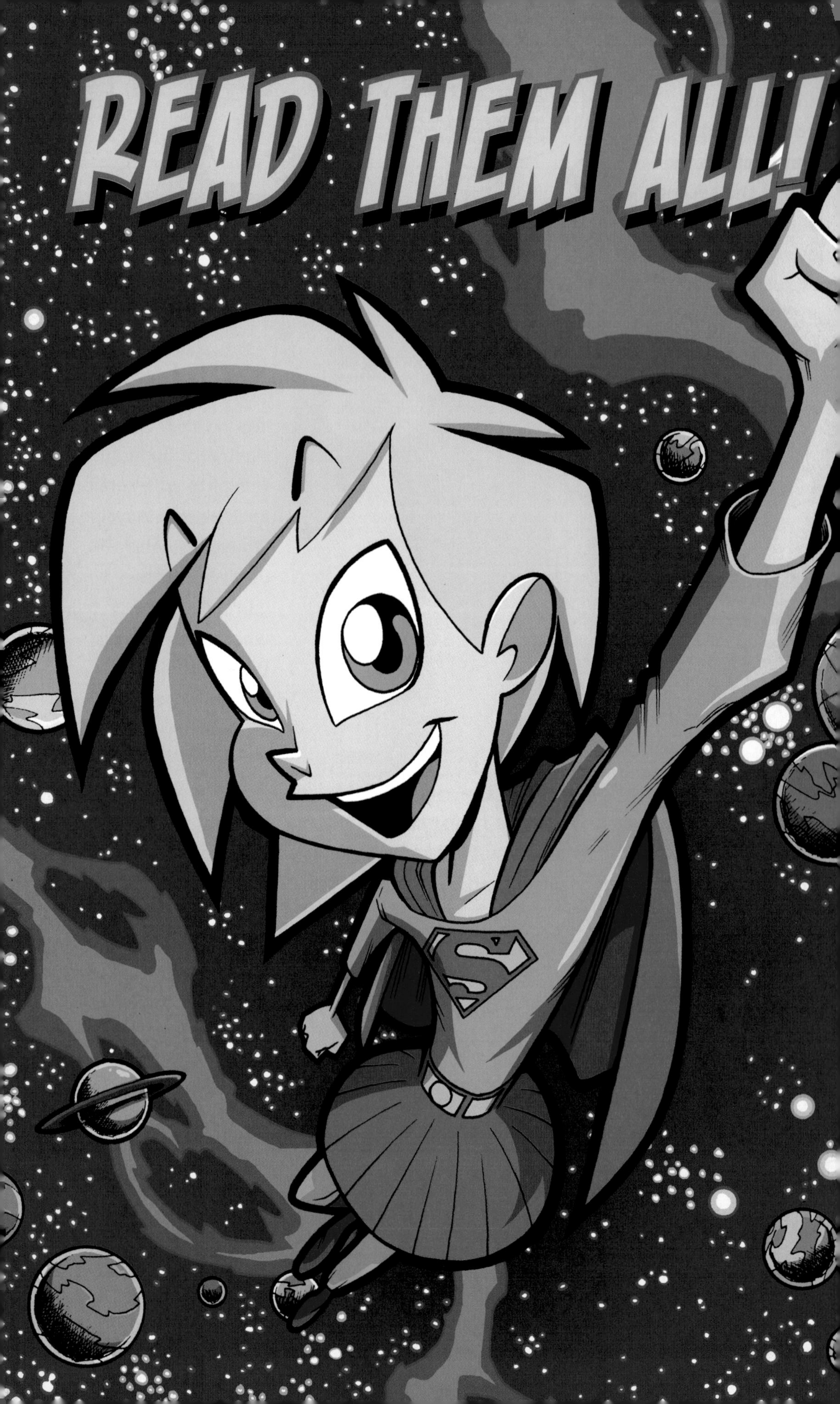
READ THEM ALL!

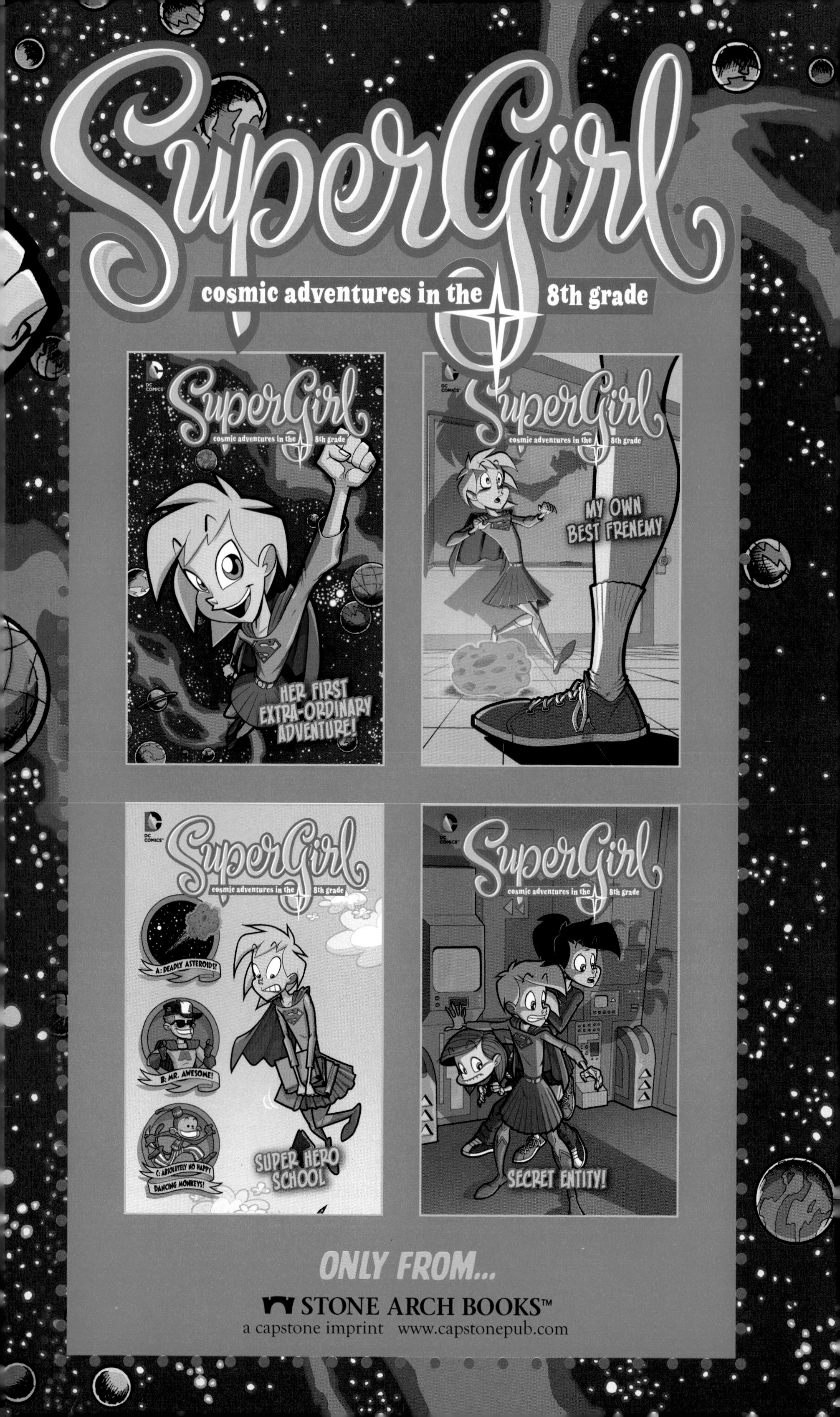
SuperGirl
cosmic adventures in the 8th grade
DC COMICS
SuperGirl
cosmic adventures in the 8th grade
HER FIRST EXTRA-ORDINARY ADVENTURE!
DC COMICS
SuperGirl
cosmic adventures in the 8th grade
MY OWN BEST FRENEMY
DC COMICS
SuperGirl
cosmic adventures in the 8th grade
A: DEADLY ASTEROIDS!
B: MR. AWESOME!
C: ABSOLUTELY NO HAPPY DANCING MONKEYS!
SUPER HERO SCHOOL
DC COMICS
SuperGirl
cosmic adventures in the 8th grade
SECRET ENTITY!
ONLY FROM...
STONE ARCH BOOKS™
a capstone imprint www.capstonepub.com

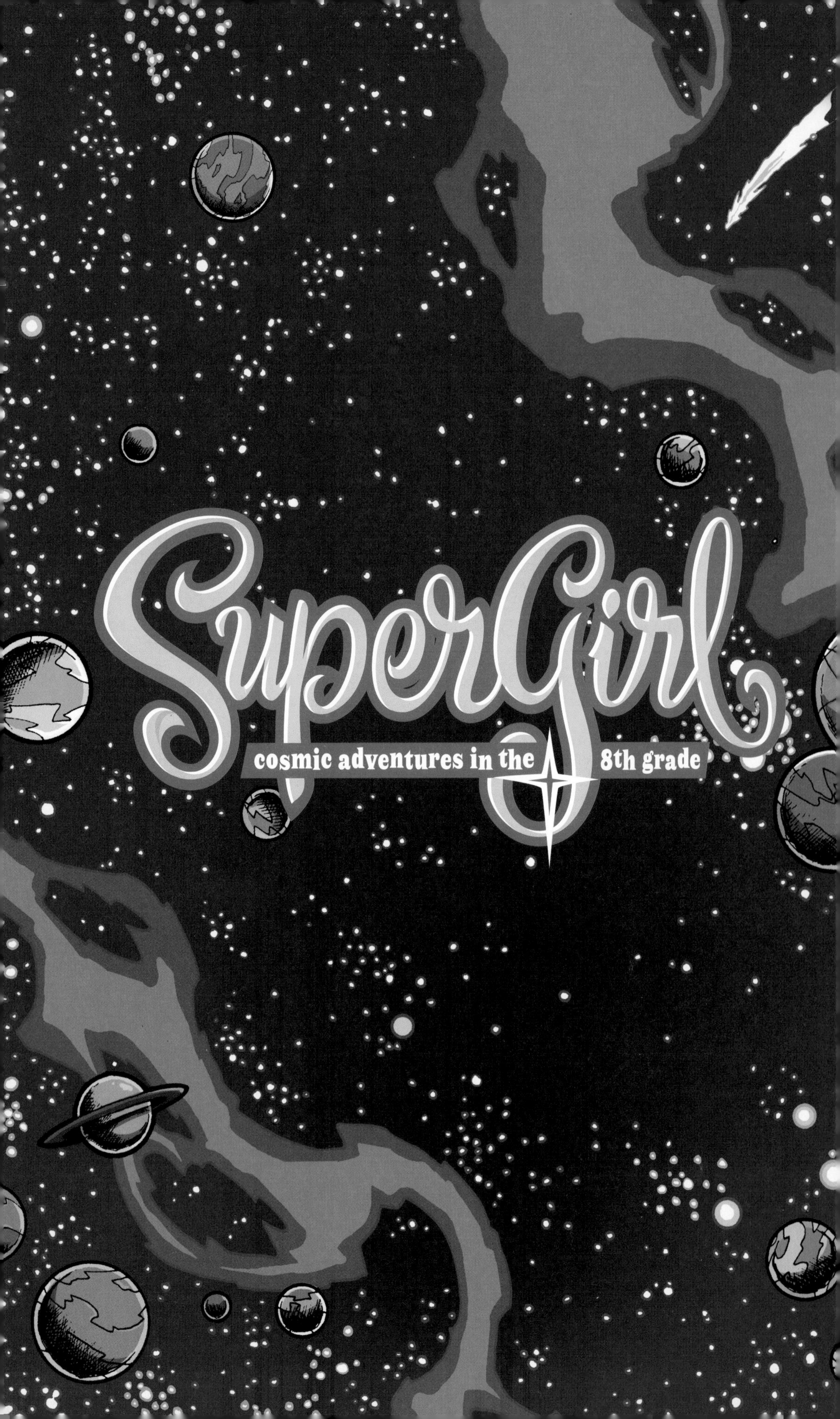
SuperGirl
cosmic adventures in the 8th grade